CHRISTMAS
WITH ANNE

Other Collections of L.M. Montgomery
Stories Edited by Rea Wilmshurst

LUCY MAUD MONTGOMERY

CHRISTMAS WITH ANNE

and Other Holiday Stories

Edited by Rea Wilmshurst

Delacorte Press

Published by
Delacorte Press
Bantam Doubleday Dell Publishing Group, Inc.
1540 Broadway
New York, New York 10036

Contents

Introduction

When I discovered in 1977, at Lucy Maud Montgomery's birthplace at Clifton Corners, P.E.I., a cache of twelve scrapbooks of her stories, I was delighted. I had been a fan of Montgomery's all my life, and thought I had read absolutely everything she had written. But these were stories I had never seen before! It was like Christmas in mid-summer. Over the next few years I had all the scrapbooks copied, and while I was compiling a bibliography of the titles – getting the names of the magazines they appeared in and the dates they were published – I discovered even more stories by Montgomery that she had never put in her scrapbooks. Then her son Dr. Stuart Macdonald gave me the list she kept of every story she ever published. It gave me the names of many other tales, and I tried to find them too. After three years' work I had a list of over five hundred.

Amongst these "rediscovered" stories – most of which have not been seen by the reading public since they first appeared around the turn of the

century – are the Christmas and New Year's tales
I have selected for this book. The magazines for
which these stories were written wanted something topical from Montgomery, tales that would
fit the season and celebrate it. Some of the magazines, too, wanted stories that would give their
readers, especially the younger ones, a message, and
if we find these tales are inclined to tack on a little
lesson or give a little sermon at the end, we must
forgive Montgomery. She did want, after all, to sell
her work, and if a few lines of homily would do it,
she would add them. More often, however, the
lesson is entwined more subtly into the story and
we pick it up only subconsciously.

While considering a book of Montgomery's
Christmas and New Year's stories, I also thought
of the Anne books. Can anyone who has read *Anne
of Green Gables* forget her joy at receiving her first
beautiful dress on Christmas morning? Marilla had
always kept Anne warmly and serviceably gowned,
but the dresses were not fashionable, to say the least.
Then Matthew, watching a group of Anne's
schoolmates, realizes that something is different
about the way she is dressed. Could it be the sleeves
of her dress? He takes the problem to Mrs. Lynde,
who offers to make up a lovely new dress for Anne,
and in the latest fashion. When Matthew unwraps
its tissue paper swathings on Christmas morning,

Anne weeps with delight. And with new evening slippers from Miss Barry she is able to take part in the school concert, secure and confident in the possession of her new and beautiful clothes.

This is one of the most heart-warming chapters in all the Anne books, and perhaps it is the spirit of Christmas that makes it so. We realize that Matthew is as delighted in giving his gift as Anne is in receiving it.

In each of these tales we meet the wide range of characters that Montgomery always supplies. The many eccentric old ladies; the wise older women who gently guide younger people to an understanding of the spirit of Christmas; the young people of various conditions, bored because they always receive too many gifts, or desperate because they have absolutely no money to buy presents for others; the many children, some waiting for Santa Claus under adverse conditions but confident that he will come, and others wanting to share the little they have. Montgomery doesn't want to break our hearts with sad stories, so these tales end happily. But the progress to the happy ending can wring tears from us. It is this combination of shadow and sunshine, of sadness and happiness, and the nostalgia for a more pleasant past, that has enabled many people like me to read Montgomery's stories and novels over and over again for many years.

To keep Anne in the picture, I have also included "Katherine Brooke Comes to Green Gables," from *Anne of Windy Poplars*. Anne, grown up now, is the principal at Summerside High School, and persuades the reluctant Katherine to return with her to Green Gables for the holidays.

Montgomery's Christmas and New Year's tales seemed to link naturally with the Anne Christmas chapters, so our theme became Christmas with Anne and other holiday stories. The spirit of giving to others is strong in these tales and may provide modern youngsters reading them with another way to look at this holiday season.

MATTHEW INSISTS ON
PUFFED SLEEVES

Matthew was having a bad ten minutes of it. He had come into the kitchen, in the twilight of a cold, grey December evening, and had sat down in the wood-box corner to take off his heavy boots, unconscious of the fact that Anne and a bevy of her schoolmates were having a practice of "The Fairy Queen" in the sitting-room. Presently they came trooping through the hall and out into the kitchen, laughing and chattering gaily. They did not see Matthew, who shrank bashfully back into the shadows beyond the wood-box with a boot in one hand and a bootjack in the other, and he watched them shyly for the aforesaid ten minutes as they put on caps and jackets and talked about the dialogue and the concert. Anne stood among them, bright-eyed and animated as they; but Matthew suddenly became conscious that there was something about her different from her mates. And what worried Matthew was that the difference impressed him as being something that should not exist. Anne had a brighter face, and bigger, starrier eyes, and more delicate features than the others; even shy, unobservant Matthew had learned to take note of these things; but the difference that disturbed him did not consist in any of these respects. Then in what did it consist?

Matthew was haunted by this question long after the girls had gone, arm in arm, down the long, hard-frozen lane and Anne had betaken herself to her books. He could not refer it to Marilla, who, he felt, would be quite sure to sniff scornfully and remark that the only difference she saw between Anne and the other girls was that they sometimes kept their tongues quiet while Anne never did. This, Matthew felt, would be no great help.

He had recourse to his pipe that evening to help him study it out, much to Marilla's disgust. After two hours of smoking and hard reflection Matthew arrived at a solution of his problem. Anne was not dressed like the other girls!

The more Matthew thought about the matter the more he was convinced that Anne never had been dressed like the other girls – never since she had come to Green Gables. Marilla kept her clothed in plain, dark dresses, all made after the same unvarying pattern. If Matthew knew there was such a thing as fashion in dress it is as much as he did; but he was quite sure that Anne's sleeves did not look at all like the sleeves the other girls wore. He recalled the cluster of little girls he had seen around her that evening – all gay in waists of red and blue and pink and white – and he wondered why Marilla always kept her so plainly and soberly gowned.

Of course, it must be all right. Marilla knew best and Marilla was bringing her up. Probably some wise, inscrutable motive was to be served thereby. But surely it would do no harm to let the child have one pretty dress – something like Diana Barry always wore. Matthew decided that he would give her one; that surely could not be objected to as an unwarranted putting in of his oar. Christmas was only a fortnight off. A nice new dress would be the very thing for a present. Matthew, with a sigh of satisfaction, put away his pipe and went to bed, while Marilla opened all the doors and aired the house.

The very next evening Matthew betook himself to Carmody to buy the dress, determined to get the worst over and have done with it. It would be, he felt assured, no trifling ordeal. There were some things Matthew could buy and prove himself no mean bargainer; but he knew he would be at the mercy of shopkeepers when it came to buying a girl's dress.

After much cogitation Matthew resolved to go to Samuel Lawson's store instead of William Blair's. To be sure, the Cuthberts always had gone to William Blair's; it was almost as much a matter of conscience with them as to attend the Presbyterian church and vote Conservative. But William Blair's two daughters frequently waited on customers there and Matthew held them in absolute dread. He could contrive to deal with them when he knew exactly what he wanted and could point it out; but in such a matter as this, requiring explanation and consultation, Matthew felt that he must be sure of a man behind the counter. So he would go to Lawson's, where Samuel or his son would wait on him.

Alas! Matthew did not know that Samuel, in the recent expansion of his business, had set up a lady clerk also; she was a niece of his wife's and a very dashing young person indeed, with a huge, drooping pompadour, big, rolling brown eyes, and a most extensive and bewildering smile. She was dressed with exceeding smartness and wore several bangle bracelets that glittered and rattled and tinkled with every movement of her hands. Matthew was covered with confusion at finding her there at all; and those bangles completely wrecked his wits at one fell swoop.

"What can I do for you this evening, Mr. Cuthbert?" Miss Lucilla Harris inquired, briskly and ingratiatingly, tapping the counter with both hands.

"Have you any – any – any – well now, say any garden rakes?" stammered Matthew.

Miss Harris looked somewhat surprised, as well she might, to hear a man inquiring for garden rakes in the middle of December.

"I believe we have one or two left over," she said, "but they're upstairs in the lumber-room. I'll go and see."

During her absence Matthew collected his scattered senses for another effort.

When Miss Harris returned with the rake and cheerfully inquired: "Anything else tonight, Mr. Cuthbert?" Matthew took his courage in both hands and replied: "Well now, since you suggest it, I might as well – take – that is – look at – buy some – some hayseed."

Miss Harris had heard Matthew Cuthbert called odd. She now concluded that he was entirely crazy.

"We only keep hayseed in the spring," she explained loftily. "We've none on hand just now."

"Oh, certainly – certainly – just as you say,"

stammered unhappy Matthew, seizing the rake
and making for the door. At the threshold he
recollected that he had not paid for it and he turned
miserably back. While Miss Harris was counting
out his change he rallied his powers for a final desperate attempt.

"Well now – if it isn't too much trouble – I
might as well – that is – I'd like to look at – at –
some sugar."

"White or brown?" queried Miss Harris
patiently.

"Oh – well now – brown," said Matthew feebly.

"There's a barrel of it over there," said Miss
Harris, shaking her bangles at it. "It's the only kind
we have."

"I'll – I'll take twenty pounds of it," said
Matthew, with beads of perspiration standing on his
forehead.

Matthew had driven halfway home before he
was his own man again. It had been a gruesome
experience, but it served him right, he thought,
for committing the heresy of going to a strange
store. When he reached home he hid the rake in the
tool-house, but the sugar he carried in to Marilla.

"Brown sugar!" exclaimed Marilla. "Whatever
possessed you to get so much? You know I never
use it except for the hired man's porridge or black
fruit-cake. Jerry's gone and I've made my cake long

ago. It's not good sugar, either – it's coarse and dark – William Blair doesn't usually keep sugar like that."

"I – I thought it might come in handy some-time," said Matthew, making good his escape.

When Matthew came to think the matter over he decided that a woman was required to cope with the situation. Marilla was out of the question. Matthew felt sure she would throw cold water on his project at once. Remained only Mrs. Lynde; for of no other woman in Avonlea would Matthew have dared to ask advice. To Mrs. Lynde he went accordingly, and that good lady promptly took the matter out of the harassed man's hands.

"Pick out a dress for you to give Anne? To be sure I will. I'm going to Carmody tomorrow and I'll attend to it. Have you something particular in mind? No? Well, I'll just go by my own judgment then. I believe a nice rich brown would just suit Anne, and William Blair has some new gloria in that's real pretty. Perhaps you'd like me to make it up for her, too, seeing that if Marilla was to make it Anne would probably get wind of it before the time and spoil the surprise? Well, I'll do it. No, it isn't a mite of trouble. I like sewing. I'll make it to fit my niece, Jenny Gillis, for she and Anne are as like as two peas as far as figure goes."

"Well now, I'm much obliged," said Matthew, "and – and – I dunno – but I'd like – I think they make the sleeves different nowadays to what they used to be. If it wouldn't be asking too much I – I'd like them made in the new way."

"Puffs? Of course. You needn't worry a speck more about it, Matthew. I'll make it up in the very latest fashion," said Mrs. Lynde. To herself she added when Matthew had gone:

"It'll be a real satisfaction to see that poor child wearing something decent for once. The way Marilla dresses her is positively ridiculous, that's what, and I've ached to tell her so plainly a dozen times. I've held my tongue though, for I can see Marilla doesn't want advice and she thinks she knows more about bringing children up than I do for all she's an old maid. But that's always the way. Folks that has brought up children know that there's no hard and fast method in the world that'll suit every child. But them as never have think it's all as plain and easy as Rule of Three – just set your three terms down so fashion, and the sum'll work out correct. But flesh and blood don't come under the head of arithmetic and that's where Marilla Cuthbert makes her mistake. I suppose she's trying to cultivate a spirit of humility in Anne by dressing her as she does; but it's more likely to cultivate envy and discontent. I'm sure the child must feel the difference between her clothes and the other girls'. But to think of Matthew taking notice of it! That man is waking up after being asleep for over sixty years."

Marilla knew all the following fortnight that Matthew had something on his mind, but what it was she could not guess, until Christmas Eve, when Mrs. Lynde brought up the new dress. Marilla behaved pretty well on the whole, although it is very likely she distrusted Mrs. Lynde's diplomatic explanation that she had made the dress because Matthew was afraid Anne would find out about it too soon if Marilla made it.

"So this is what Matthew has been looking so mysterious over and grinning about to himself for two weeks, is it?" she said a little stiffly but tolerantly. "I knew he was up to some foolishness. Well, I must say I don't think Anne needed any more dresses. I made her three good, warm, serviceable ones this fall, and anything more is sheer extravagance. There's enough material in those sleeves alone to make a waist, I declare there is. You'll just pamper Anne's vanity, Matthew, and she's as vain as a peacock now. Well, I hope she'll be satisfied at last, for I know she's been hankering after those silly sleeves ever since they came in, although she never said a word after the first. The puffs have been getting bigger and more ridiculous right along;

they're as big as balloons now. Next year anybody who wears them will have to go through a door sideways."

Christmas morning broke on a beautiful white world. It had been a very mild December and people had looked forward to a green Christmas; but just enough snow fell softly in the night to transfigure Avonlea. Anne peeped out from her frosted gable window with delighted eyes. The firs in the Haunted Wood were all feathery and wonderful; the birches and wild cherry trees were outlined in pearl; the ploughed fields were stretches of snowy dimples; and there was a crisp tang in the air that was glorious. Anne ran downstairs singing until her voice re-echoed through Green Gables.

"Merry Christmas, Marilla! Merry Christmas, Matthew! Isn't it a lovely Christmas? I'm so glad it's white. Any other kind of Christmas doesn't seem real, does it? I don't like green Christmases. They're *not* green — they're just nasty faded browns and greys. What makes people call them green? Why — why — Matthew, is that for me? Oh, Matthew!"

Matthew had sheepishly unfolded the dress from its paper swathings and held it out with a deprecatory glance at Marilla, who feigned to be contemptuously filling the teapot, but nevertheless watched the scene out of the corner of her eye with a rather interested air.

Anne took the dress and looked at it in reverent silence. Oh, how pretty it was – a lovely soft brown gloria with all the gloss of silk; a skirt with dainty frills and shirrings; a waist elaborately pintucked in the most fashionable way, with a little ruffle of filmy lace at the neck. But the sleeves – they were the crowning glory! Long elbow cuffs, and above them two beautiful puffs divided by rows of shirring and bows of brown silk ribbon.

"That's a Christmas present for you, Anne," said Matthew shyly. "Why – why – Anne, don't you like it? Well now – well now."

For Anne's eyes had suddenly filled with tears.

"*Like* it! Oh, Matthew!" Anne laid the dress over a chair and clasped her hands. "Matthew, it's perfectly exquisite. Oh, I can never thank you enough. Look at those sleeves! Oh, it seems to me this must be a happy dream."

"Well, well, let us have breakfast," interrupted Marilla. "I must say, Anne, I don't think you needed the dress; but since Matthew has got it for you, see that you take good care of it. There's a hair ribbon Mrs. Lynde left for you. It's brown, to match the dress. Come now, sit in."

"I don't see how I'm going to eat breakfast," said Anne rapturously. "Breakfast seems so commonplace at such an exciting moment. I'd rather feast my eyes on that dress. I'm so glad that puffed sleeves are still fashionable. It did seem to me that I'd never get over it if they went out before I had a dress with them. I'd never have felt quite satisfied, you see. It was lovely of Mrs. Lynde to give me the ribbon, too. I feel that I ought to be a very good girl indeed. It's at times like this I'm sorry I'm not a model little girl; and I always resolve that I will be in future. But somehow it's hard to carry out your resolutions when irresistible temptations come. Still, I really will make an extra effort after this."

When the commonplace breakfast was over Diana appeared, crossing the white log bridge in the hollow, a gay little figure in her crimson ulster. Anne flew down the slope to meet her.

"Merry Christmas, Diana! And oh, it's a wonderful Christmas. I've something splendid to show you. Matthew has given me the loveliest dress, with *such* sleeves. I couldn't even imagine any nicer."

"I've got something more for you," said Diana breathlessly. "Here – this box. Aunt Josephine sent us out a big box with ever so many things in it – and this is for you. I'd have brought it over last night, but it didn't come until after dark, and I never feel very comfortable coming through the Haunted Wood in the dark now."

Anne opened the box and peeped in. First a card with "For the Anne-girl and Merry Christmas," written on it; and then, a pair of the daintiest little kid slippers, with beaded toes and satin bows and glistening buckles.

"Oh," said Anne, "Diana, this is too much. I must be dreaming."

"*I* call it providential," said Diana. "You won't have to borrow Ruby's slippers now, and that's a blessing, for they're two sizes too big for you, and it would be awful to hear a fairy shuffling. Josie Pye would be delighted. Mind you, Rob Wright went home with Gertie Pye from the practice night before last. Did you ever hear anything equal to that?"

All the Avonlea scholars were in a fever of excitement that day, for the hall had to be decorated and a last grand rehearsal held.

The concert came off in the evening and was a pronounced success. The little hall was crowded; all the performers did excellently well, but Anne was the bright particular star of the occasion, as even envy, in the shape of Josie Pye, dared not deny.

"Oh, hasn't it been a brilliant evening?" sighed Anne, when it was all over and she and Diana were walking home together under a dark, starry sky.

"Everything went off very well," said Diana practically. "I guess we must have made as much as ten dollars. Mind you, Mr. Allan is going to send an account of it to the Charlottetown papers."

"Oh, Diana, will we really see our names in

print? It makes me thrill to think of it. Your solo was perfectly elegant, Diana. I felt prouder than you did when it was encored. I just said to myself, 'It is my dear bosom friend who is so honoured.'"

"Well, your recitations just brought down the house, Anne. That sad one was simply splendid."

"Oh, I was so nervous, Diana. When Mr. Allan called out my name I really cannot tell how I ever got up on that platform. I felt as if a million eyes were looking at me and through me, and for one dreadful moment I was sure I couldn't begin at all. Then I thought of my lovely puffed sleeves and took courage. I knew that I must live up to those sleeves, Diana. So I started in, and my voice seemed to be coming from ever so far away. I just felt like a parrot. It's providential that I practised those recitations so often up in the garret, or I'd never have been able to get through. Did I groan all right?"

"Yes, indeed, you groaned lovely," assured Diana.

"I saw old Mrs. Sloane wiping away tears when I sat down. It was splendid to think I had touched somebody's heart. It's so romantic to take part in a concert, isn't it? Oh, it's been a very memorable occasion indeed."

"Wasn't the boys' dialogue fine?" said Diana. "Gilbert Blythe was just splendid. Anne, I do think it's awful mean the way you treat Gil. Wait till I tell

Matthew Insists on Puffed Sleeves

you. When you ran off the platform after the fairy dialogue one of your roses fell out of your hair. I saw Gil pick it up and put it in his breast pocket. There now. You're so romantic that I'm sure you ought to be pleased at that."

"It's nothing to me what that person does," said Anne loftily. "I simply never waste a thought on him, Diana."

That night Marilla and Matthew, who had been out to a concert for the first time in twenty years, sat for awhile by the kitchen fire after Anne had gone to bed.

"Well now, I guess our Anne did as well as any of them," said Matthew proudly.

"Yes, she did," admitted Marilla. "She's a bright child, Matthew. And she looked real nice, too. I've been kind of opposed to this concert scheme, but I suppose there's no real harm in it after all. Anyhow, I was proud of Anne tonight, although I'm not going to tell her so."

"Well now, I was proud of her and I did tell her so 'fore she went upstairs," said Matthew. "We must see what we can do for her some of these days, Marilla. I guess she'll need something more than Avonlea school by and by."

"There's time enough to think of that," said Marilla. "She's only thirteen in March. Though tonight it struck me she was growing quite a big girl. Mrs. Lynde made that dress a mite too long, and it makes Anne look so tall. She's quick to learn and I guess the best thing we can do for her will be to send her to Queen's after a spell. But nothing need be said about that for a year or two yet."

"Well now, it'll do no harm to be thinking it over off and on," said Matthew. "Things like that are all the better for lots of thinking over."

CHRISTMAS AT RED BUTTE

O f course Santa Claus will come," said Jimmy Martin confidently. Jimmy was ten, and at ten it is easy to be confident. "Why, he's *got* to come because it is Christmas Eve, and he always *has* come. You know that, twins."

Yes, the twins knew it and, cheered by Jimmy's superior wisdom, their doubts passed away. There had been one terrible moment when Theodora had sighed and told them they mustn't be too much disappointed if Santa Claus did not come this year because the crops had been poor, and he mightn't have had enough presents to go around.

"That doesn't make any difference to Santa Claus," scoffed Jimmy. "You know as well as I do, Theodora Prentice, that Santa Claus is rich whether the crops fail or not. They failed three years ago, before Father died, but Santa Claus came all the same. Prob'bly you don't remember it, twins, 'cause you were too little, but I do. Of course he'll come, so don't you worry a mite. And he'll bring my skates and your dolls. He knows we're expecting them, Theodora, 'cause we wrote him a letter last week, and threw it up the chimney. And there'll be candy and nuts, of course, and Mother's gone to town to buy a turkey. I tell you we're going to have a ripping Christmas."

"Well, don't use such slangy words about it, Jimmy-boy," sighed Theodora. She couldn't bear to dampen their hopes any further, and perhaps Aunt Elizabeth might manage it if the colt sold well. But Theodora had her painful doubts, and she sighed again as she looked out of the window far down the trail that wound across the prairie, red-lighted by the declining sun of the short wintry afternoon.

"Do people always sigh like that when they get to be sixteen?" asked Jimmy curiously. "You didn't sigh like that when you were only fifteen, Theodora. I wish you wouldn't. It makes me feel funny – and it's not a nice kind of funniness either."

"It's a bad habit I've got into lately," said Theodora, trying to laugh. "Old folks are dull sometimes, you know, Jimmy-boy."

"Sixteen *is* awful old, isn't it?" said Jimmy reflectively. "I'll tell you what *I'm* going to do when I'm

sixteen, Theodora. I'm going to pay off the mort-
gage, and buy mother a silk dress, and a piano for
the twins. Won't that be elegant? I'll be able to do
that 'cause I'm a man. Of course if I was only a
girl I couldn't."

"I hope you'll be a good kind brave man and a
real help to your mother," said Theodora softly,
sitting down before the cosy fire and lifting the fat
little twins into her lap.

"Oh, I'll be good to her, never you fear," assured
Jimmy, squatting comfortably down on the little fur
rug before the stove – the skin of the coyote his
father had killed four years ago. "I believe in being
good to your mother when you've only got the
one. Now tell us a story, Theodora – a real jolly
story, you know, with lots of fighting in it. Only
please don't kill anybody. I like to hear about fighting, but I like to have all the people come out alive."

Theodora laughed, and began a story about the
Riel Rebellion of '85 – a story which had the
double merit of being true and exciting at the same
time. It was quite dark when she finished, and the
twins were nodding, but Jimmy's eyes were wide
open and sparkling.

"That was great," he said, drawing a long breath.
"Tell us another."

"No, it's bedtime for you all," said Theodora
firmly. "One story at a time is my rule, you know."

"But I want to sit up till Mother comes home," objected Jimmy.

"You can't. She may be very late, for she would have to wait to see Mr. Porter. Besides, you don't know what time Santa Claus might come – if he comes at all. If he were to drive along and see you children up instead of being sound asleep in bed, he might go right on and never call at all."

This argument was too much for Jimmy.

"All right, we'll go. But we have to hang up our stockings first. Twins, get yours."

The twins toddled off in great excitement, and brought back their Sunday stockings, which Jimmy proceeded to hang along the edge of the mantel shelf. This done, they all trooped obediently off to bed. Theodora gave another sigh, and seated herself at the window, where she could watch the moonlit prairie for Mrs. Martin's homecoming and knit at the same time.

I am afraid that you will think from all the sighing Theodora was doing that she was a very melancholy and despondent young lady. You couldn't think anything more unlike the real Theodora. She was the jolliest, bravest girl of sixteen in all Saskatchewan, as her shining brown eyes and rosy, dimpled cheeks would have told you; and her sighs were not on her own account, but simply for fear the children were going to be disappointed. She knew that they would be almost heartbroken if Santa Claus did not come, and that this would hurt the patient hardworking little mother more than all else.

Five years before this, Theodora had come to live with Uncle George and Aunt Elizabeth in the little log house at Red Butte. Her own mother had just died, and Theodora had only her big brother Donald left, and Donald had Klondike fever. The Martins were poor, but they had gladly made room for their little niece, and Theodora had lived there ever since, her aunt's right-hand girl and the beloved playmate of the children. They had been very happy until Uncle George's death two years before this Christmas Eve; but since then there had been hard times in the little log house, and though Mrs. Martin and Theodora did their best, it was a woefully hard task to make both ends meet, especially this year when their crops had been poor. Theodora and her aunt had made every sacrifice possible for the children's sake, and at least Jimmy and the twins had not felt the pinch very severely yet.

At seven Mrs. Martin's bells jingled at the door and Theodora flew out. "Go right in and get warm, Auntie," she said briskly. "I'll take Ned away and unharness him."

"It's a bitterly cold night," said Mrs. Martin

wearily. There was a note of discouragement in her voice that struck dismay to Theodora's heart.

"I'm afraid it means no Christmas for the children tomorrow," she thought sadly, as she led Ned away to the stable. When she returned to the kitchen Mrs. Martin was sitting by the fire, her face in her chilled hands, sobbing convulsively.

"Auntie – oh, Auntie, don't!" exclaimed Theodora impulsively. It was such a rare thing to see her plucky, resolute little aunt in tears. "You're cold and tired – I'll have a nice cup of tea for you in a trice."

"No, it isn't that," said Mrs. Martin brokenly. "It was seeing those stockings hanging there. Theodora, I couldn't get a thing for the children – not a single thing. Mr. Porter would only give forty dollars for the colt, and when all the bills were paid there was barely enough left for such necessaries as we must have. I suppose I ought to feel thankful I could get those. But the thought of the children's disappointment tomorrow is more than I can bear. It would have been better to have told them long ago, but I kept building on getting more for the colt. Well, it's weak and foolish to give way like this. We'd better both take a cup of tea and go to bed. It will save fuel."

When Theodora went up to her little room her face was very thoughtful. She took a small box from her table and carried it to the window. In it was a very pretty little gold locket hung on a narrow blue ribbon. Theodora held it tenderly in her fingers, and looked out over the moonlit prairie with a very sober face. Could she give up her dear locket – the locket Donald had given her just before he started for the Klondike? She had never thought she could do such a thing. It was almost the only thing she had to remind her of Donald – handsome, merry, impulsive, warmhearted Donald, who had gone away four years ago with a smile on his bonny face and splendid hope in his heart.

"Here's a locket for you, Gift o' God," he had said gaily – he had such a dear loving habit of calling her by the beautiful meaning of her name. A lump came into Theodora's throat as she remembered it. "I couldn't afford a chain too, but when I come back I'll bring you a rope of Klondike nuggets for it."

Then he had gone away. For two years letters had come from him regularly. Then he wrote that he had joined a prospecting party to a remote wilderness. After that was silence, deepening into anguish of suspense that finally ended in hopelessness. A rumour came that Donald Prentice was dead. None had returned from the expedition he had joined. Theodora had long ago given up all hope of ever seeing Donald again. Hence her locket was doubly dear to her.

But Aunt Elizabeth had always been so good and loving and kind to her. Could she not make the sacrifice for her sake? Yes, she could and would. Theodora flung up her head with a gesture that meant decision. She took out of the locket the bits of hair – her mother's and Donald's – which it contained (perhaps a tear or two fell as she did so) and then hastily donned her warmest cap and wraps. It was only three miles to Spencer; she could easily walk it in an hour and, as it was Christmas Eve, the shops would be open late. She must walk, for Ned could not be taken out again, and the mare's foot was sore. Besides, Aunt Elizabeth must not know until it was done.

As stealthily as if she were bound on some nefarious errand, Theodora slipped downstairs and out of the house. The next minute she was hurrying along the trail in the moonlight. The great dazzling prairie was around her, the mystery and splendour of the northern night all about her. It was very calm and cold, but Theodora walked so briskly that she kept warm. The trail from Red Butte to Spencer was a lonely one. Mr. Lurgan's house, halfway to town, was the only dwelling on it.

When Theodora reached Spencer she made her way at once to the only jewellery store the little town contained. Mr. Benson, its owner, had been a friend of her uncle's, and Theodora felt sure that he would buy her locket. Nevertheless her heart beat quickly, and her breath came and went uncomfortably fast as she went in. Suppose he wouldn't buy it. Then there would be no Christmas for the children at Red Butte.

"Good evening, Miss Theodora," said Mr. Benson briskly. "What can I do for you?"

"I'm afraid I'm not a very welcome sort of customer, Mr. Benson," said Theodora, with an uncertain smile. "I want to sell, not buy. Could you – will you buy this locket?"

Mr. Benson pursed up his lips, took up the locket, and examined it. "Well, I don't often buy second-hand stuff," he said, after some reflection, "but I don't mind obliging you, Miss Theodora. I'll give you four dollars for this trinket."

Theodora knew the locket had cost a great deal more than that, but four dollars would get what she wanted, and she dared not ask for more. In a few minutes the locket was in Mr. Benson's possession, and Theodora, with four crisp new bills in her purse, was hurrying to the toy store. Half an hour later she was on her way back to Red Butte, with as many parcels as she could carry – Jimmy's skates, two lovely dolls for the twins, packages of nuts and candy, and a nice plump turkey. Theodora beguiled her lonely tramp by picturing the children's joy in the morning.

About a quarter of a mile past Mr. Lurgan's house the trail curved suddenly about a bluff of poplars. As Theodora rounded the turn she halted in amazement. Almost at her feet the body of a man was lying across the road. He was clad in a big fur coat, and had a fur cap pulled well down over his forehead and ears. Almost all of him that could be seen was a full bushy beard. Theodora had no idea who he was, or where he had come from. But she realized that he was unconscious, and that he would speedily freeze to death if help were not brought. The footprints of a horse galloping across the prairie suggested a fall and a runaway, but Theodora did not waste time in speculation. She ran back at full speed to Mr. Lurgan's, and roused the household. In a few minutes Mr. Lurgan and his son had hitched a horse to a wood-sleigh, and hurried down the trail to the unfortunate man.

Theodora, knowing that her assistance was not needed, and that she ought to get home as quickly as possible, went on her way as soon as she had seen the stranger in safe keeping. When she reached the little log house she crept in, cautiously put the children's gifts in their stockings, placed the turkey on the table where Aunt Elizabeth would see it the first thing in the morning, and then slipped off to bed, a very weary but very happy girl.

The joy that reigned in the little log house the next day more than repaid Theodora for her sacrifice.

"Whoopee, didn't I tell you that Santa Claus would come all right!" shouted the delighted Jimmy. "Oh, what splendid skates!"

The twins hugged their dolls in silent rapture, but Aunt Elizabeth's face was the best of all.

Then the dinner had to be prepared, and everybody had a hand in that. Just as Theodora, after a grave peep into the oven, had announced that the turkey was done, a sleigh dashed around the house. Theodora flew to answer the knock at the door, and there stood Mr. Lurgan and a big, bewhiskered, fur-coated fellow whom Theodora recognized as the stranger she had found on the trail. But – *was* he a stranger? There was something oddly familiar in those merry brown eyes. Theodora felt herself growing dizzy.

"Donald!" she gasped. "Oh, Donald!"

And then she was in the big fellow's arms, laughing and crying at the same time.

Donald it was indeed. And then followed half an hour during which everybody talked at once, and the turkey would have been burned to a crisp had it not been for the presence of mind of Mr. Lurgan who, being the least excited of them all, took it out of the oven, and set it on the back of the stove.

"To think that it was you last night, and that I never dreamed it," exclaimed Theodora. "Oh, Donald, if I hadn't gone to town!"

"I'd have frozen to death, I'm afraid," said Donald soberly. "I got into Spencer on the last train last night. I felt that I must come right out – I couldn't wait till morning. But there wasn't a team to be got for love or money – it was Christmas Eve and all the livery rigs were out. So I came on horseback. Just by that bluff something frightened my horse, and he shied violently. I was half asleep and thinking of my little sister, and I went off like a shot. I suppose I struck my head against a tree. Anyway, I knew nothing more until I came to in Mr. Lurgan's kitchen. I wasn't much hurt – feel none the worse of it except for a sore head and shoulder. But, oh, Gift o' God, how you have grown! I can't realize that you are the little sister I left four years ago. I suppose you have been thinking I was dead?"

"Yes, and, oh, Donald, where *have* you been?"

"Well, I went way up north with a prospecting party. We had a tough time the first year, I can tell you, and some of us never came back. We weren't in a country where post offices were lying round loose either, you see. Then at last, just as we were about giving up in despair, we struck it rich. I've brought a snug little pile home with me, and things are going to look up in this log house, Gift o' God. There'll be no more worrying for you dear people over mortgages."

"I'm so glad – for Auntie's sake," said Theodora, with shining eyes. "But, oh, Donald, it's best of all just to have you back. I'm so perfectly happy that I don't know what to do or say."

"Well, I think you might have dinner," said Jimmy in an injured tone. "The turkey's getting stone cold, and I'm most starving. I just can't stand it another minute."

So, with a laugh, they all sat down to the table and ate the merriest Christmas dinner the little log house had ever known.

THE END OF THE YOUNG
FAMILY FEUD

A week before Christmas, Aunt Jean wrote to Elizabeth, inviting her and Alberta and me to eat our Christmas dinner at Monkshead. We accepted with delight. Aunt Jean and Uncle Norman were delightful people, and we knew we should have a jolly time at their house. Besides, we wanted to see Monkshead, where Father had lived in his boyhood, and the old Young homestead where he had been born and brought up and where Uncle William still lived. Father never said much about it, but we knew he loved it very dearly, and we had always greatly desired to get at least a glimpse of what Alberta liked to call "our ancestral halls."

Since Monkshead was only sixty miles away, and Uncle William lived there as aforesaid, it may be pertinently asked what there was to prevent us from visiting it and the homestead as often as we wished. We answer promptly: the family feud.

Father and Uncle William were on bad terms, or rather on no terms at all, and had been ever since we could remember. After Grandfather Young's death there had been a wretched quarrel over the property. Father always said that he had been as much to blame as Uncle William, but Great-aunt Emily told us that Uncle William had been by far the most to blame, and that he had behaved scandalously to Father. Moreover, she said that Father had gone to him when cooling-down time came, apologized for what he had said, and asked Uncle William to be friends again; and that William simply turned his back on Father and walked into the house without saying a word, but, as Great-aunt Emily said, with the Young temper sticking out of every kink and curve of his figure. Great-aunt Emily is our aunt on Mother's side, and she does not like any of the Youngs except Father and Uncle Norman.

This was why we had never visited Monkshead. We had never seen Uncle William, and we always thought of him as a sort of ogre when we thought of him at all. When we were children, our old nurse, Margaret Hannah, used to frighten us into good behaviour by saying ominously, "If you 'uns aint good your Uncle Willlam'll cotch you."

What he would do to us when he "cotched" us she never specified, probably reasoning that the unknown was always more terrible than the known. My private opinion in those days was that he would boil us in oil and pick our bones.

Uncle Norman and Aunt Jean had been living out west for years. Three months before this Christmas they had come east, bought a house in Monkshead, and settled there. They had been down to see us, and Father and Mother and the boys had been up to see them, but we three girls had not; so we were pleasantly excited at the thought of spending Christmas there.

Christmas morning was fine, white as a pearl and clear as a diamond. We had to go by the seven o'clock train, since there was no other before eleven, and we reached Monkshead at eight-thirty.

When we stepped from the train the station-master asked us if we were the three Miss Youngs. Alberta pleaded guilty, and he said, "Well, here's a letter for you then."

We took the letter and went into the waiting room with sundry misgivings. What had happened? Were Uncle Norman and Aunt Jean quarantined for scarlet fever, or had burglars raided the pantry

and carried off the Christmas supplies? Elizabeth
opened and read the letter aloud. It was from Aunt
Jean to the following effect:

> DEAR GIRLS: I am so sorry to disappoint you,
> but I cannot help it. Word has come from
> Streatham that my sister has met with a serious
> accident and is in a very critical condition. Your
> uncle and I must go to Streatham immediately
> and are leaving on the eight o'clock express. I
> know you have started before this, so there is no
> use in telegraphing. We want you to go right to
> the house and make yourself at home. You will
> find the key under the kitchen doorstep, and the
> dinner in the pantry all ready to cook. There are
> two mince pies on the third shelf, and the plum
> pudding only needs to be warmed up. You will
> find a little Christmas remembrance for each of
> you on the dining-room table. I hope you will
> make as merry as you possibly can and we will
> have you down again as soon as we come back.
> Your hurried and affectionate,
> AUNT JEAN

We looked at each other somewhat dolefully.
But, as Alberta pointed out, we might as well make
the best of it, since there was no way of getting
home before the five o'clock train. So we trailed

out to the stationmaster, and asked him limply if he could direct us to Mr. Norman Young's house.

He was a rather grumpy individual, very busy with pencil and notebook over some freight; but he favoured us with his attention long enough to point with his pencil and say jerkily, "Young's? See that red house on the hill? That's it."

The red house was about a quarter of a mile from the station, and we saw it plainly. Accordingly, to the red house we betook ourselves. On nearer view it proved to be a trim, handsome place, with nice grounds and very fine old trees.

We found the key under the kitchen doorstep and went in. The fire was black out, and somehow things wore a more cheerless look than I had expected to find. I may as well admit that we marched into the dining room first of all, to find our presents.

There were three parcels, two very small and one pretty big, lying on the table, but when we came to look for names there were none.

"Evidently Aunt Jean, in her hurry and excitement, forgot to label them," said Elizabeth. "Let us open them. We may be able to guess from the contents which belongs to whom."

I must say we were surprised when we opened those parcels. We had known that Aunt Jean's gifts would be nice, but we had not expected anything like this. There was a magnificent stone marten collar, a dear little gold watch and pearl chatelaine, and a gold chain bracelet set with turquoises.

"The collar must be for you, Elizabeth, because Mary and I have one already, and Aunt Jean knows it," said Alberta; "the watch must be for you, Mary, because I have one; and by the process of exhaustion the bracelet must be for me. Well, they are all perfectly sweet."

Elizabeth put on her collar and paraded in front of the sideboard mirror. It was so dusty she had to take her handkerchief and wipe it before she could see herself properly. Everything in the room was equally dusty. As for the lace curtains, they looked as if they hadn't been washed for years, and one of them had a long ragged hole in it. I couldn't help feeling secretly surprised, for Aunt Jean had the reputation of being a perfect housekeeper. However, I didn't say anything, and neither did the other girls. Mother had always impressed upon us that it was the height of bad manners to criticize anything we might not like in a house where we were guests.

"Well, let's see about dinner," said Alberta, practically, snapping her bracelet on her wrist and admiring the effect.

We went to the kitchen, where Elizabeth proceeded to light the fire, that being one of her specialties, while Alberta and I explored the pantry. We found the dinner supplies laid out as Aunt Jean had explained. There was a nice fat turkey all stuffed, and vegetables galore. The mince pies were in their place, but they were almost the only things about which that could be truthfully said, for the disorder of that pantry was enough to give a tidy person nightmares for a month. "I never in all my life saw – " began Alberta, and then stopped short, evidently remembering Mother's teaching.

"Where is the plum pudding?" said I, to turn the conversation into safer channels.

It was nowhere to be seen, so we concluded it must be in the cellar. But we found the cellar door padlocked good and fast.

"Never mind," said Elizabeth. "You know none of us really likes plum pudding. We only eat it because it is the proper traditional dessert. The mince pies will suit us better."

We hurried the turkey into the oven, and soon everything was going merrily. We had lots of fun getting up that dinner, and we made ourselves perfectly at home, as Aunt Jean had commanded. We kindled a fire in the dining room and dusted everything in sight. We couldn't find anything remotely resembling a duster, so we used our handkerchiefs. When we got through, the room looked like something, for the furnishings were really very handsome, but our handkerchiefs – well!

Then we set the table with all the nice dishes we could find. There was only one long tablecloth in the sideboard drawer, and there were three holes in it, but we covered them with dishes and put a little potted palm in the middle for a centrepiece. At one o'clock dinner was ready for us and we for it. Very nice that table looked, too, as we sat down to it.

Just as Alberta was about to spear the turkey with a fork and begin carving, that being one of *her* specialties, the kitchen door opened and somebody walked in. Before we could move, a big, handsome, bewhiskered man in a fur coat appeared in the dining-room doorway.

I wasn't frightened. He seemed quite respectable, I thought, and I supposed he was some intimate friend of Uncle Norman's. I rose politely and said, "Good day."

You never saw such an expression of amazement as was on that poor man's face. He looked from me to Alberta and from Alberta to Elizabeth and from Elizabeth to me again as if he doubted the evidence of his eyes.

"Mr. and Mrs. Norman Young are not at home," I explained, pitying him. "They went to Streatham this morning because Mrs. Young's sister is very ill."

"What does all this mean?" said the big man gruffly. "This isn't Norman Young's house . . . it is mine. I'm William Young. Who are you? And what are you doing here?"

I fell back into my chair, speechless. My very first impulse was to put up my hand and cover the gold watch. Alberta had dropped the carving knife and was trying desperately to get the gold bracelet off under the table. In a flash we had realized our mistake and its awfulness. As for me, I felt positively frightened; Margaret Hannah's warnings of old had left an ineffaceable impression.

Elizabeth rose to the occasion. Rising to the occasion is another of Elizabeth's specialties. Besides, she was not hampered by the tingling consciousness that she was wearing a gift that had not been intended for her.

"We have made a mistake, I fear," she said, with a dignity which I appreciated even in my panic, "and we are very sorry for it. We were invited to spend Christmas with Mr. and Mrs. Norman Young. When we got off the train we were given a letter from them stating that they were summoned away but telling us to go to their house and make ourselves at home. The stationmaster told us that this was the house, so we came here. We have never been in Monkshead, so we did not know the difference. Please pardon us."

I had got off the watch by this time and laid it on the table, unobserved, as I thought. Alberta, not having the key of the bracelet, had not been able to get it off, and she sat there crimson with shame. As for Uncle William, there was positively a twinkle in his eye. He did not look in the least ogreish.

"Well, it has been quite a fortunate mistake for me," he said. "I came home expecting to find a cold house and a raw dinner, and I find this instead. I'm very much obliged to you."

Alberta rose, went to the mantel piece, took the key of the bracelet therefrom, and unlocked it. Then she faced Uncle William. "Mrs. Young told us in her letter that we would find our Christmas gifts on the table, so we took it for granted that these things belonged to us," she said desperately. "And now, if you will kindly tell us where Mr. Norman Young does live, we won't intrude on you any longer. Come, girls."

Elizabeth and I rose with a sigh. There was nothing else to be done, of course, but we were fearfully hungry, and we did not feel enthusiastic over the prospect of going to another empty house and cooking another dinner.

"Wait a bit," said Uncle William. "I think since you have gone to all the trouble of cooking the dinner it's only fair you should stay and help to eat it. Accidents seem to be rather fashionable just now. My housekeeper's son broke his leg down at Weston, and I had to take her there early this morning. Come, introduce yourselves. To whom am I indebted for this pleasant surprise?"

"We are Elizabeth, Alberta, and Mary Young of Green Village," I said; and then I looked to see the ogre creep out if it were ever going to.

But Uncle William merely looked amazed for the first moment, foolish for the second, and the third he was himself again.

"Robert's daughters?" he said, as if it were the most natural thing in the world that Robert's daughters should be there in his house. "So you are my nieces? Well, I'm very glad to make your acquaintance. Sit down and we'll have dinner as soon as I can get my coat off. I want to see if you are as good cooks as your mother used to be long ago."

We sat down, and so did Uncle William. Alberta had her chance to show what she could do at carving, for Uncle William said it was something he never did; he kept a housekeeper just for that. At first we felt a bit stiff and awkward; but that soon wore off, for Uncle William was genial, witty, and entertaining. Soon, to our surprise, we found that we were enjoying ourselves. Uncle William seemed to be, too. When we had finished he leaned back and looked at us.

"I suppose you've been brought up to abhor me and all my works?" he said abruptly.

"Not by Father and Mother," I said frankly.
"They never said anything against you. Margaret
Hannah did, though. She brought us up in the way
we should go through fear of you."

Uncle William laughed.

"Margaret Hannah was a faithful old enemy of
mine," he said. "Well, I acted like a fool – and
worse. I've been sorry for it ever since. I was in the
wrong. I couldn't have said this to your father, but
I don't mind saying it to you, and you can tell him
if you like."

"He'll be delighted to hear that you are no
longer angry with him," said Alberta. "He has
always longed to be friends with you again, Uncle
William. But he thought you were still bitter against
him."

"No – no – nothing but stubborn pride," said
Uncle William. "Now, girls, since you are my
guests I must try to give you a good time. We'll take
the double sleigh and have a jolly drive this afternoon. And about those trinkets there – they are
yours. I did get them for some young friends of
mine here, but I'll give them something else. I
want you to have these. That watch looked very
nice on your blouse, Mary, and the bracelet became
Alberta's pretty wrist very well. Come and give
your cranky old uncle a hug for them."

Uncle William got his hugs heartily; then we washed up the dishes and went for our drive. We got back just in time to catch the evening train home. Uncle William saw us off at the station, under promise to come back and stay a week with him when his housekeeper came home.

"One of you will have to come and stay with me altogether, pretty soon," he said. "Tell your father he must be prepared to hand over one of his girls to me as a token of his forgiveness. I'll be down to talk it over with him shortly."

When we got home and told our story, Father said, "Thank God!" very softly. There were tears in his eyes. He did not wait for Uncle William to come down, but went to Monkshead himself the next day.

In the spring Alberta is to go and live with Uncle William. She is making a supply of dusters now. And next Christmas we are going to have a grand family reunion at the old homestead. Mistakes are not always bad.

AUNT CYRILLA'S
CHRISTMAS BASKET

hen Lucy Rose met Aunt Cyrilla coming downstairs, somewhat flushed and breathless from her ascent to the garret, with a big, flat-covered basket hanging over her plump arm, she gave a little sigh of despair. Lucy Rose had done her brave best for some years – in fact, ever since she had put up her hair and lengthened her skirts – to break Aunt Cyrilla of the habit of carrying that basket with her every time she went to Pembroke; but Aunt Cyrilla still insisted on taking it, and only laughed at what she called Lucy Rose's "finicky notions." Lucy Rose had a horrible, haunting idea that it was extremely provincial for her aunt always to take the big basket, packed full of country good things, whenever she went to visit Edward and Geraldine. Geraldine was so stylish, and might think it queer; and then Aunt Cyrilla always would carry it on her arm and give cookies and apples and molasses taffy out of it to every child she encountered and, just as often as not, to older folks too. Lucy Rose, when she went to town with Aunt Cyrilla, felt chagrined over this – all of which goes to prove that Lucy was as yet very young and had a great deal to learn in this world.

That troublesome worry over what Geraldine would think nerved her to make a protest in this instance.

"Now, Aunt C'rilla," she pleaded, "you're surely not going to take that funny old basket to Pembroke this time – Christmas Day and all."

"'Deed and 'deed I am," returned Aunt Cyrilla briskly, as she put it on the table and proceeded to dust it out. "I never went to see Edward and Geraldine since they were married that I didn't take a basket of good things along with me for them, and I'm not going to stop now. As for it's being Christmas, all the more reason. Edward is always real glad to get some of the old farmhouse goodies. He says they beat city cooking all hollow, and so they do."

"But it's so countrified," moaned Lucy Rose.

"Well, I am countrified," said Aunt Cyrilla firmly, "and so are you. And what's more, I don't see that it's anything to be ashamed of. You've got some real silly pride about you, Lucy Rose. You'll grow out of it in time, but just now it is giving you a lot of trouble."

"The basket is a lot of trouble," said Lucy Rose crossly. "You're always mislaying it or afraid you will. And it does look so funny to be walking through the streets with that big, bulgy basket hanging on your arm."

"I'm not a mite worried about its looks," returned Aunt Cyrilla calmly. "As for its being a trouble, why, maybe it is, but I have that, and other people have the pleasure of it. Edward and Geraldine don't need it – I know that – but there may be those that will. And if it hurts your feelings to walk 'longside of a countrified old lady with a countrified basket, why, you can just fall behind, as it were."

Aunt Cyrilla nodded and smiled good-humouredly, and Lucy Rose, though she privately held to her own opinion, had to smile too.

"Now, let me see," said Aunt Cyrilla reflectively, tapping the snowy kitchen table with the point of her plump, dimpled forefinger, "what shall I take? That big fruit cake for one thing – Edward does like my fruit cake; and that cold boiled tongue for another. Those three mince pies too, they'd spoil before we got back or your uncle'd make himself sick eating them – mince pie is his besetting sin. And that little stone bottle full of cream – Geraldine

may carry any amount of style, but I've yet to see
her look down on real good country cream, Lucy
Rose; and another bottle of my raspberry vinegar.
That plate of jelly cookies and doughnuts will
please the children and fill up the chinks, and you
can bring me that box of ice-cream candy out of
the pantry, and that bag of striped candy sticks your
uncle brought home from the corner last night.
And apples, of course – three or four dozen of
those good eaters – and a little pot of my greengage
preserves – Edward'll like that. And some sandwiches and pound cake for a snack for ourselves.
Now, I guess that will do for eatables. The presents
for the children can go in on top. There's a doll
for Daisy and the little boat your uncle made for
Ray and a tatted lace handkerchief apiece for the
twins, and the crochet hood for the baby. Now, is
that all?"

"There's a cold roast chicken in the pantry," said
Lucy Rose wickedly, "and the pig Uncle Leo killed
is hanging up in the porch. Couldn't you put them
in too?"

Aunt Cyrilla smiled broadly. "Well, I guess we'll
leave the pig alone; but since you have reminded me
of it, the chicken may as well go in. I can make
room."

Lucy Rose, in spite of her prejudices, helped
with the packing and, not having been trained

under Aunt Cyrilla's eye for nothing, did it very well too, with much clever economy of space. But when Aunt Cyrilla had put in as a finishing touch a big bouquet of pink and white everlastings, and tied the bulging covers down with a firm hand, Lucy Rose stood over the basket and whispered vindictively:

"Some day I'm going to burn this basket – when I get courage enough. Then there'll be an end of lugging it everywhere we go like a – like an old market-woman."

Uncle Leopold came in just then, shaking his head dubiously. He was not going to spend Christmas with Edward and Geraldine, and perhaps the prospect of having to cook and eat his Christmas dinner all alone made him pessimistic.

"I mistrust you folks won't get to Pembroke tomorrow," he said sagely. "It's going to storm."

Aunt Cyrilla did not worry over this. She believed matters of this kind were fore-ordained, and she slept calmly. But Lucy Rose got up three times in the night to see if it were storming, and when she did sleep had horrible nightmares of struggling through blinding snowstorms dragging Aunt Cyrilla's Christmas basket along with her.

It was not snowing in the early morning, and Uncle Leopold drove Aunt Cyrilla and Lucy Rose and the basket to the station, four miles off. When they reached there the air was thick with flying flakes. The stationmaster sold them their tickets with a grim face.

"If there's any more snow comes, the trains might as well keep Christmas too," he said. "There's been so much snow already that traffic is blocked half the time, and now there ain't no place to shovel the snow off onto."

Aunt Cyrilla said that if the train were to get to Pembroke in time for Christmas, it would get there; and she opened her basket and gave the stationmaster and three small boys an apple apiece.

"That's the beginning," groaned Lucy Rose to herself.

When their train came along Aunt Cyrilla established herself in one seat and her basket in another, and looked beamingly around her at her fellow travellers.

These were few in number — a delicate little woman at the end of the car, with a baby and four other children, a young girl across the aisle with a pale, pretty face, a sunburned lad three seats ahead in a khaki uniform, a very handsome, imposing old lady in a sealskin coat ahead of him, and a thin young man with spectacles opposite.

"A minister," reflected Aunt Cyrilla, beginning to classify, "who takes better care of other folks' souls than of his own body; and that woman in the sealskin is discontented and cross at something – got up too early to catch the train, maybe; and that young chap must be one of the boys not long out of the hospital. That woman's children look as if they hadn't enjoyed a square meal since they were born; and if that girl across from me has a mother, I'd like to know what the woman means, letting her daughter go from home in this weather in clothes like that."

Lucy Rose merely wondered uncomfortably what the others thought of Aunt Cyrilla's basket.

They expected to reach Pembroke that night, but as the day wore on the storm grew worse. Twice the train had to stop while the train hands dug it out. The third time it could not go on. It was dusk when the conductor came through the train, replying brusquely to the questions of the anxious passengers.

"A nice lookout for Christmas – no, impossible to go on or back – track blocked for miles – what's that, madam? – no, no station near – woods for miles. We're here for the night. These storms of late have played the mischief with everything."

"Oh, dear," groaned Lucy Rose.

Aunt Cyrilla looked at her basket complacently. "At any rate, we won't starve," she said.

The pale, pretty girl seemed indifferent. The sealskin lady looked crosser than ever. The khaki boy said, "Just my luck," and two of the children began to cry. Aunt Cyrilla took some apples and striped candy sticks from her basket and carried them to them. She lifted the oldest into her ample lap and soon had them all around her, laughing and contented.

The rest of the travellers straggled over to the corner and drifted into conversation. The khaki boy said it was hard lines not to get home for Christmas, after all.

"I was invalided from South Africa three months ago, and I've been in the hospital at Netley ever since. Reached Halifax three days ago and telegraphed the old folks I'd eat my Christmas dinner with them, and to have an extra-big turkey because I didn't have any last year. They'll be badly disappointed."

He looked disappointed too. One khaki sleeve hung empty by his side. Aunt Cyrilla passed him an apple.

"We were all going down to Grandpa's for Christmas," said the little mother's oldest boy dolefully. "We've never been there before, and it's just too bad."

He looked as if he wanted to cry but thought better of it and bit off a mouthful of candy.

"Will there be any Santa Claus on the train?" demanded his small sister tearfully. "Jack says there won't."

"I guess he'll find you out," said Aunt Cyrilla reassuringly.

The pale, pretty girl came up and took the baby from the tired mother. "What a dear little fellow," she said softly.

"Are you going home for Christmas too?" asked Aunt Cyrilla.

The girl shook her head. "I haven't any home. I'm just a shop girl out of work at present, and I'm going to Pembroke to look for some."

Aunt Cyrilla went to her basket and took out her box of cream candy. "I guess we might as well enjoy ourselves. Let's eat it all up and have a good time. Maybe we'll get down to Pembroke in the morning."

The little group grew cheerful as they nibbled, and even the pale girl brightened up. The little mother told Aunt Cyrilla her story aside. She had been long estranged from her family, who had disapproved of her marriage. Her husband had died the previous summer, leaving her in poor circumstances

"Father wrote to me last week and asked me to let bygones be bygones and come home for Christmas. I was so glad. And the children's hearts were set on it. It seems too bad that we are not to get there. I have to be back at work the morning after Christmas."

The khaki boy came up again and shared the candy. He told amusing stories of campaigning in South Africa. The minister came too, and listened, and even the sealskin lady turned her head over her shoulder.

By and by the children fell asleep, one on Aunt Cyrilla's lap and one on Lucy Rose's, and two on the seat. Aunt Cyrilla and the pale girl helped the mother make up beds for them. The minister gave his overcoat and the sealskin lady came forward with a shawl.

"This will do for the baby," she said.

"We must get up some Santa Claus for these youngsters," said the khaki boy. "Let's hang their stockings on the wall and fill 'em up as best we can. I've nothing about me but some hard cash and a jack-knife. I'll give each of 'em a quarter and the boy can have the knife."

"I've nothing but money either," said the sealskin lady regretfully.

Aunt Cyrilla glanced at the little mother. She had fallen asleep with her head against the seat-back.

"I've got a basket over there," said Aunt Cyrilla firmly, "and I've some presents in it that I was taking to my nephew's children. I'm going to give 'em to these. As for the money, I think the mother is the one for it to go to. She's been telling me her story, and a pitiful one it is. Let's make up a little purse among us for a Christmas present."

The idea met with favour. The khaki boy passed his cap and everybody contributed. The sealskin lady put in a crumpled note. When Aunt Cyrilla straightened it out she saw that it was for twenty dollars.

Meanwhile, Lucy Rose had brought the basket. She smiled at Aunt Cyrilla as she lugged it down the aisle and Aunt Cyrilla smiled back. Lucy Rose had never touched that basket of her own accord before.

Ray's boat went to Jacky, and Daisy's doll to his oldest sister, the twins' lace handkerchiefs to the two smaller girls and the hood to the baby. Then the stockings were filled up with doughnuts and jelly cookies and the money was put in an envelope and pinned to the little mother's jacket.

"That baby is such a dear little fellow," said the sealskin lady gently. "He looks something like my little son. He died eighteen Christmases ago."

Aunt Cyrilla put her hand over the lady's kid glove. "So did mine," she said. Then the two women smiled tenderly at each other. Afterwards they rested from their labours and all had what Aunt Cyrilla called a "snack" of sandwiches and pound cake. The khaki boy said he hadn't tasted anything half so good since he left home.

"They didn't give us pound cake in South Africa," he said

When morning came the storm was still raging. The children wakened and went wild with delight over their stockings. The little mother found her envelope and tried to utter thanks and broke down; and nobody knew what to say or do, when the conductor fortunately came in and made a diversion by telling them they might as well resign themselves to spending Christmas on the train.

"This is serious," said the khaki boy, "when you consider that we've no provisions. Don't mind for myself, used to half rations or no rations at all. But these kiddies will have tremendous appetites."

Then Aunt Cyrilla rose to the occasion.

"I've got some emergency rations here," she announced. "There's plenty for all and we'll have our Christmas dinner, although a cold one. Breakfast first thing. There's a sandwich apiece left and we must fill up on what is left of the cookies and doughnuts and save the rest for a real good spread at dinner time. The only thing is, I haven't any bread."

"I've a box of soda crackers," said the little mother eagerly

Nobody in that car will ever forget that Christmas. To begin with, after breakfast they had a concert. The khaki boy gave two recitations, sang three songs, and gave a whistling solo. Lucy Rose gave three recitations and the minister a comic reading. The pale shop girl sang two songs. It was agreed that the khaki boy's whistling solo was the best number, and Aunt Cyrilla gave him the bouquet of everlastings as a reward of merit.

Then the conductor came in with the cheerful news that the storm was almost over and he thought the track would be cleared in a few hours.

"If we can get to the next station we'll be all right," he said. "The branch joins the main line there and the tracks will be clear."

At noon they had dinner. The train hands were invited in to share it. The minister carved the chicken with the brakeman's jack-knife and the khaki boy cut up the tongue and the mince pies, while the sealskin lady mixed the raspberry vinegar with its due proportion of water. Bits of paper served as plates. The train furnished a couple of glasses, a tin pint cup was discovered and given to the children, Aunt Cyrilla and Lucy Rose and the sealskin lady drank, turn about, from the latter's

graduated medicine glass, the shop girl and the little
mother shared one of the empty bottles, and the
khaki boy, the minister, and the train men drank
out of the other bottle.

Everybody declared they had never enjoyed a
meal more in their lives. Certainly it was a merry
one, and Aunt Cyrilla's cooking was never more
appreciated; indeed, the bones of the chicken and
the pot of preserves were all that was left. They
could not eat the preserves because they had no
spoons, so Aunt Cyrilla gave them to the little
mother.

When all was over, a hearty vote of thanks was
passed to Aunt Cyrilla and her basket. The sealskin lady wanted to know how she made her pound
cake, and the khaki boy asked for her receipt for
jelly cookies. And when two hours later the conductor came in and said the snowploughs had got
along and they'd soon be starting, they all wondered
if it could really be less than twenty-four hours
since they met.

"I feel as if I'd been campaigning with you all
my life," said the khaki boy.

At the next station they all parted. The little
mother and the children had to take the next train
back home. The minister stayed there, and the
khaki boy and the sealskin lady changed trains. The

sealskin lady shook Aunt Cyrilla's hand. She no longer looked discontented or cross.

"This has been the pleasantest Christmas I have ever spent," she said heartily. "I shall never forget that wonderful basket of yours. The little shop girl is going home with me. I've promised her a place in my husband's store."

When Aunt Cyrilla and Lucy Rose reached Pembroke there was nobody to meet them because everyone had given up expecting them. It was not far from the station to Edward's house and Aunt Cyrilla elected to walk.

"I'll carry the basket," said Lucy Rose.

Aunt Cyrilla relinquished it with a smile. Lucy Rose smiled too.

"It's a blessed old basket," said the latter, "and I love it. Please forget all the silly things I ever said about it, Aunt C'rilla."

THE OSBORNES' CHRISTMAS

ousin Myra had come to spend Christmas at "The Firs," and all the junior Osbornes were ready to stand on their heads with delight. Darby – whose real name was Charles – did it, because he was only eight, and at eight you have no dignity to keep up. The others, being older, couldn't.

But the fact of Christmas itself awoke no great enthusiasm in the hearts of the junior Osbornes. Frank voiced their opinion of it the day after Cousin Myra had arrived. He was sitting on the table with his hands in his pockets and a cynical sneer on his face. At least, Frank flattered himself that it was cynical. He knew that Uncle Edgar was said to wear a cynical sneer, and Frank admired Uncle Edgar very much and imitated him in every possible way. But to you and me it would have

looked just as it did to Cousin Myra – a very discontented and unbecoming scowl.

"I'm awfully glad to see you, Cousin Myra,"
explained Frank carefully, "and your being here
may make some things worth while. But Christmas
is just a bore – a regular bore."

That was what Uncle Edgar called things that
didn't interest him, so that Frank felt pretty sure of
his word. Nevertheless, he wondered uncomfortably what made Cousin Myra smile so queerly.

"Why, how dreadful!" she said brightly. "I
thought all boys and girls looked upon Christmas as
the very best time in the year."

"We don't," said Frank gloomily. "It's just the
same old thing year in and year out. We know just
exactly what is going to happen. We even know
pretty well what presents we are going to get. And
Christmas Day itself is always the same. We'll get
up in the morning, and our stockings will be full
of things, and half of them we don't want. Then
there's dinner. It's always so poky. And all the
uncles and aunts come to dinner – just the same
old crowd, every year, and they say just the same
things. Aunt Desda always says, 'Why, Frankie,
how you have grown!' She knows I hate to be
called Frankie. And after dinner they'll sit round
and talk the rest of the day, and that's all. Yes, I call
Christmas a nuisance."

"There isn't a single bit of fun in it," said Ida discontentedly.

"Not a bit!" said the twins, both together, as they always said things.

"There's lots of candy," said Darby stoutly. He rather liked Christmas, although he was ashamed to say so before Frank.

Cousin Myra smothered another of those queer smiles.

"You've had too much Christmas, you Osbornes," she said seriously. "It has palled on your taste, as all good things will if you overdo them. Did you ever try giving Christmas to somebody else?"

The Osbornes looked at Cousin Myra doubtfully. They didn't understand.

"We always send presents to all our cousins," said Frank hesitatingly. "That's a bore, too. They've all got so many things already it's no end of bother to think of something new."

"That isn't what I mean," said Cousin Myra. "How much Christmas do you suppose those little Rolands down there in the hollow have? Or Sammy Abbott with his lame back? Or French Joe's family over the hill? If you have too much Christmas, why don't you give some to them?"

The Osbornes looked at each other. This was a new idea.

"How could we do it?" asked Ida.

Whereupon they had a consultation. Cousin Myra explained her plan, and the Osbornes grew enthusiastic over it. Even Frank forgot that he was supposed to be wearing a cynical sneer.

"I move we do it, Osbornes," said he.

"If Father and Mother are willing," said Ida.

"Won't it be jolly!" exclaimed the twins.

"Well, rather," said Darby scornfully. He did not mean to be scornful. He had heard Frank saying the same words in the same tone, and thought it signified approval.

Cousin Myra had a talk with Father and Mother Osborne that night, and found them heartily in sympathy with her plans.

For the next week the Osbornes were agog with excitement and interest. At first Cousin Myra made the suggestions, but their enthusiasm soon outstripped her, and they thought out things for themselves. Never did a week pass so quickly. And the Osbornes had never had such fun, either.

Christmas morning there was not a single present given or received at "The Firs" except those which Cousin Myra and Mr. and Mrs. Osborne gave to each other. The junior Osbornes had asked that the money which their parents had planned to spend in presents for them be given to them the previous week; and given it was, without a word.

The uncles and aunts arrived in due time, but

not with them was the junior Osbornes' concern. They were the guests of Mr. and Mrs. Osborne. The junior Osbornes were having a Christmas dinner party of their own. In the small dining room a table was spread and loaded with good things. Ida and the twins cooked that dinner all by themselves. To be sure, Cousin Myra had helped some, and Frank and Darby had stoned all the raisins and helped pull the home-made candy; and all together they had decorated the small dining room royally with Christmas greens.

Then their guests came. First, all the little Rolands from the Hollow arrived – seven in all, with very red, shining faces and not a word to say for themselves, so shy were they. Then came a troop from French Joe's – four black-eyed lads, who never knew what shyness meant. Frank drove down to the village in the cutter and brought lame Sammy back with him, and soon after the last guest arrived – little Tillie Mather, who was Miss Rankin's "orphan 'sylum girl" from over the road. Everybody knew that Miss Rankin never kept Christmas. She did not believe in it, she said, but she did not prevent Tillie from going to the Osbornes' dinner party.

Just at first the guests were a little stiff and un-social; but they soon got acquainted, and so jolly was Cousin Myra – who had her dinner with the children in preference to the grown-ups – and so

friendly the junior Osbornes, that all stiffness vanished. What a merry dinner it was! What peals of
laughter went up, reaching to the big dining room
across the hall, where the grown-ups sat in rather
solemn state. And how those guests did eat and
frankly enjoy the good things before them! How
nicely they all behaved, even to the French Joes!
Myra had secretly been a little dubious about those
four mischievous-looking lads, but their manners
were quite flawless. Mrs. French Joe had been
drilling them for three days – ever since they had
been invited to "de Chrismus dinner at de beeg
house."

After the merry dinner was over, the junior
Osbornes brought in a Christmas tree, loaded with
presents. They had bought them with the money
that Mr. and Mrs. Osborne had meant for their
own presents, and a splendid assortment they were.
All the French-Joe boys got a pair of skates apiece,
and Sammy a set of beautiful books, and Tillie was
made supremely happy with a big wax doll. Every
little Roland got just what his or her small heart had
been longing for. Besides, there were nuts and
candies galore.

Then Frank hitched up his pony again, but this
time into a great pung sleigh, and the junior
Osbornes took their guests for a sleigh-drive, chap-
eroned by Cousin Myra. It was just dusk when they

got back, having driven the Rolands and the French Joes and Sammy and Tillie to their respective homes.

"This has been the jolliest Christmas I ever spent," said Frank, emphatically.

"I thought we were just going to give the others a good time, but it was they who gave it to us," said Ida.

"Weren't the French Joes jolly?" giggled the twins. "Such cute speeches as they would make!"

"Me and Teddy Roland are going to be chums after this," announced Darby. "He's an inch taller than me, but I'm wider."

That night Frank and Ida and Cousin Myra had a little talk after the smaller Osbornes had been haled off to bed.

"We're not going to stop with Christmas, Cousin Myra," said Frank, at the end of it. "We're just going to keep on through the year. We've never had such a delightful old Christmas before."

"You've learned the secret of happiness," said Cousin Myra gently.

And the Osbornes understood what she meant.

THE UNFORGOTTEN ONE

I t was Christmas Eve, but there was no frost, or snow, or sparkle. It was a green Christmas, and the night was mild and dim, with hazy starlight. A little wind was laughing freakishly among the firs around Ingleside and rustling among the sere grasses along the garden walks. It was more like a night in early spring or late fall than in December; but it was Christmas Eve, and there was a light in every window of Ingleside, the glow breaking out through the whispering darkness like a flame-red blossom swung against the background of the evergreens; for the children were coming home for the Christmas reunion, as they always came – Fritz and Margaret and Laddie and Nora, and Robert's two boys in the place of Robert, who had died fourteen years ago –

and the old house must put forth its best of light and good cheer to welcome them.

Doctor Fritz and his brood were the last to arrive, driving up to the hall door amid a chorus of welcoming barks from the old dogs and a hail of merry calls from the group in the open doorway.

"We're all here now," said the little mother, as she put her arms about the neck of her stalwart first-born and kissed his bearded face. There were hand-shakings and greetings and laughter. Only Nanny, far back in the shadows of the firelit hall, swallowed a resentful sob, and wiped two bitter tears from her eyes with her little red hand.

"We're not all here," she murmured under her breath. "Miss Avis isn't here. Oh, how can they be so glad? How can they have forgotten?"

But nobody heard or heeded Nanny – she was only the little orphan "help" girl at Ingleside. They were all very good to her, and they were all very fond of her, but at the times of family reunion Nanny was unconsciously counted out. There was no bond of blood to unite her to them, and she was left on the fringe of things. Nanny never resented this – it was all a matter of course to her; but on this Christmas Eve her heart was broken because she thought that nobody remembered Miss Avis.

After supper they all gathered around the open fireplace of the hall, hung with its berries and

evergreens in honour of the morrow. It was their
unwritten law to form a fireside circle on Christmas
Eve and tell each other what the year had brought
them of good and ill, sorrow and joy. The circle
was smaller by one than it had been the year before,
but none spoke of that. There was a smile on every
face and happiness in every voice.

The father and mother sat in the centre, grey-
haired and placid, their fine old faces written over
with the history of gracious lives. Beside the
mother, Doctor Fritz sat like a boy, on the floor,
with his massive head, grey as his father's, on her
lap, and one of his smooth, muscular hands, that
were as tender as a woman's at the operating table,
clasped in hers. Next to him sat sweet Nora, the
twenty-year-old "baby," who taught in a city
school; the rosy firelight gleamed lovingly over her
girlish beauty of burnished brown hair, dreamy
blue eyes, and soft, virginal curves of cheek and
throat. Doctor Fritz's spare arm was about her, but
Nora's own hands were clasped over her knee, and
on one of them sparkled a diamond that had not
been there at the last Christmas reunion. Laddie,
who figured as Archibald only in the family Bible,
sat close to the inglenook – a handsome young
fellow with a daring brow and rollicking eyes. On
the other side sat Margaret, hand in hand with her
father, a woman whose gracious sweetness of nature

enveloped her as a garment; and Robert's two laughing boys filled up the circle, looking so much alike that it was hard to say which was Cecil and which was Sid.

Margaret's husband and Fritz's wife were playing games with the children in the parlour, whence shrieks of merriment drifted out into the hall. Nanny might have been with them had she chosen, but she preferred to sit alone in the darkest corner of the hall and gaze with jealous, unhappy eyes at the mirthful group about the fire, listening to their story and jest and laughter with unavailing protest in her heart. Oh, how could they have forgotten so soon? It was not yet a full year since Miss Avis had gone. Last Christmas Eve she had sat there, a sweet and saintly presence, in the inglenook, more, so it had almost seemed, the centre of the home circle than the father and mother; and now the December stars were shining over her grave, and not one of that heedless group remembered her; not once was her name spoken; even her old dog had forgotten her – he sat with his nose in Margaret's lap, blinking with drowsy, aged contentment at the fire.

"Oh, I can't bear it!" whispered Nanny, under cover of the hearty laughter which greeted a story Doctor Fritz had been telling. She slipped out into the kitchen, put on her hood and cloak, and took

from a box under the table a little wreath of holly.
She had made it out of the bits left over from the
decorations. Miss Avis had loved holly; Miss Avis
had loved every green, growing thing.

As Nanny opened the kitchen door something
cold touched her hand, and there stood the old dog,
wagging his tail and looking up at her with wistful
eyes, mutely pleading to be taken, too.

"So you do remember her, Gyppy," said Nanny,
patting his head. "Come along then. We'll go
together."

They slipped out into the night. It was quite
dark, but it was not far to the graveyard – just out
through the evergreens and along a field by-path
and across the road. The old church was there, with
its square tower, and the white stones gleaming all
around it. Nanny went straight to a shadowy corner
and knelt on the sere grasses while she placed her
holly wreath on Miss Avis's grave. The tears in her
eyes brimmed over.

"Oh, Miss Avis! Miss Avis!" she sobbed. "I miss
you so – I miss you so! It can't ever seem like
Christmas to me without you. You were always so
sweet and kind to me. There ain't a day passes but
I think of you and all the things you used to say to
me, and I try to be good like you'd want me to be.
But I hate them for forgetting you – yes, I do! I'll

never forget you, darling Miss Avis! I'd rather be here alone with you in the dark than back there with them."

Nanny sat down by the grave. The old dog lay down by her side with his forepaws on the turf and his eyes fixed on the tall white marble shaft. It was too dark for Nanny to read the inscription but she knew every word of it: "In loving remembrance of Avis Maywood, died January 20, 1902, aged 45." And underneath the lines of her own choosing:

"Say not good night, but in some brighter clime
    Bid me good morning."

But they had forgotten her – oh, they had forgotten her already!

When half an hour had passed, Nanny was startled by approaching footsteps. Not wishing to be seen, she crept softly behind the headstones into the shadow of the willow on the farther side, and the old dog followed. Doctor Fritz, coming to the grave, thought himself alone with the dead. He knelt down by the headstone and pressed his face against it.

"Avis," he said gently, "dear Avis, I have come to visit your grave tonight because you seem nearer to me here than elsewhere. And I want to talk to you, Avis, as I have always talked to you every

Christmastide since we were children together. I have missed you so tonight, dear friend and sympathizer – no words can tell how I have missed you – your welcoming handclasp and your sweet face in the firelight shadows. I could not bear to speak your name, the aching sense of loss was so bitter. Amid all the Christmas mirth and good fellowship I felt the sorrow of your vacant chair. Avis, I wanted to tell you what the year had brought to me. My theory has been proved; it has made me a famous man. Last Christmas, Avis, I told you of it, and you listened and understood and believed in it. Dear Avis, once again I thank you for all you have been to me – all you are yet. I have brought you your roses; they are as white and pure and fragrant as your life."

Other footsteps came so quickly on Doctor Fritz' retreating ones that Nanny could not rise. It was Laddie this time – gay, careless, thoughtless Laddie.

"Roses? So Fritz has been here! I have brought you lilies, Avis. Oh, Avis, I miss you so! You were so jolly and good – you understood a fellow so well. I had to come here tonight to tell you how much I miss you. It doesn't seem half home without you. Avis, I'm trying to be a better chap – more the sort of man you'd have me be. I've given the old set the go-by – I'm trying to live up to your standard. It would be easier if you were here to help me. When I was a kid it was always easier to be good for awhile after I'd talked things over with you. I've got the best mother a fellow ever had, but you and I were such chums, weren't we, Avis? I thought I'd just break down in there tonight and put a damper on everything by crying like a baby. If anybody had spoken about you, I should have. Hello!"

Laddie wheeled around with a start, but it was only Robert's two boys, who came shyly up to the grave, half hanging back to find anyone else there.

"Hello, boys," said Laddie huskily. "So you've come to see her grave too?"

"Yes," said Cecil solemnly. "We – we just had to. We couldn't go to bed without coming. Oh, isn't it lonesome without Cousin Avis?"

"She was always so good to us," said Sid.

"She used to talk to us so nice," said Cecil chokily. "But she liked fun, too."

"Boys," said Laddie gravely, "never forget what Cousin Avis used to say to you. Never forget that you have *got* to grow up into men she'd be proud of."

They went away then, the boys and their boyish uncle; and when they had gone Nora came, stealing timidly through the shadows, starting at the rustle of the wind in the trees.

"Oh, Avis," she whispered. "I want to see you so

much! I want to tell you all about it – about *him*. You would understand so well. He is the best and dearest lover ever a girl had. You would think so too. Oh, Avis, I miss you so much! There's a little shadow even on my happiness because I can't talk it over with you in the old way. Oh, Avis, it was dreadful to sit around the fire tonight and not see you. Perhaps you were there in spirit. I love to think you were, but I wanted to see you. You were always there to come home to before, Avis, dear."

Sobbing, she went away; and then came Margaret, the grave, strong Margaret.

"Dear cousin, dear to me as a sister, it seemed to me that I must come to you here tonight. I cannot tell you how much I miss your wise, clear-sighted advice and judgment, your wholesome companionship. A little son was born to me this past year, Avis. How glad you would have been, for you knew, as none other did, the bitterness of my childless heart. How we would have delighted to talk over my baby together, and teach him wisely between us! Avis, Avis, your going made a blank that can never be filled for me!"

Margaret was still standing there when the old people came.

"Father! Mother! Isn't it too late and chilly for you to be here?"

"No, Margaret, no," said the mother. "I couldn't

go to my bed without coming to see Avis's grave.
I brought her up from a baby – her dying mother
gave her to me. She was as much my own child as
any of you. And oh! I miss her so. You only miss her
when you come home, but I miss her all the time
– every day!"

"We all miss her, Mother," said the old father,
tremulously. "She was a good girl – Avis was a good
girl. Good night, Avis!"

" 'Say not good night, but in some brighter
clime bid her good morning,' " quoted Margaret
softly. "That was her own wish, you know. Let us
go back now. It is getting late."

When they had gone Nanny crept out from the
shadows. It had not occurred to her that perhaps
she should not have listened – she had been too shy
to make her presence known to those who came to
Avis's grave. But her heart was full of joy.

"Oh, Miss Avis, I'm so glad, I'm so glad! They
haven't forgotten you after all, Miss Avis, dear, not
one of them. I'm sorry I was so cross at them; and
I'm so glad they haven't forgotten you. I love them
for it."

Then the old dog and Nanny went home
together.

CLORINDA'S GIFTS

t is a dreadful thing to be poor a fortnight before Christmas," said Clorinda, with the mournful sigh of seventeen years.

Aunt Emmy smiled. Aunt Emmy was sixty, and spent the hours she didn't spend in a bed, on a sofa or in a wheel chair; but Aunt Emmy was never heard to sigh.

"I suppose it is worse then than at any other time," she admitted.

That was one of the nice things about Aunt Emmy. She always sympathized and understood.

"I'm worse than poor this Christmas . . . I'm stony broke," said Clorinda dolefully. "My spell of fever in the summer and the consequent doctor's bills have cleaned out my coffers completely. Not a single Christmas present can I give. And I did so want to give some little thing to each of my dearest people. But I simply can't afford it . . . that's the hateful, ugly truth."

Clorinda sighed again.

"The gifts which money can purchase are not the only ones we can give," said Aunt Emmy gently, "nor the best, either."

"Oh, I know it's nicer to give something of your own work," agreed Clorinda, "but materials for fancy work cost too. That kind of gift is just as much out of the question for me as any other."

"That was not what I meant," said Aunt Emmy.

"What did you mean, then?" asked Clorinda, looking puzzled.

Aunt Emmy smiled.

"Suppose you think out my meaning for yourself," she said. "That would be better than if I explained it. Besides, I don't think I *could* explain it. Take the beautiful line of a beautiful poem to help you in your thinking out: 'The gift without the giver is bare.'"

"I'd put it the other way and say, 'The giver without the gift is bare,'" said Clorinda, with a grimace. "That is my predicament exactly. Well, I hope by next Christmas I'll not be quite bankrupt. I'm going into Mr. Callender's store down at Murraybridge in February. He has offered me the place, you know."

"Won't your aunt miss you terribly?" said Aunt Emmy gravely.

Clorinda flushed. There was a note in Aunt Emmy's voice that disturbed her.

"Oh, yes, I suppose she will," she answered hurriedly. "But she'll get used to it very soon. And I will be home every Saturday night, you know. I'm dreadfully tired of being poor, Aunt Emmy, and now that I have a chance to earn something for myself I mean to take it. I can help Aunt Mary, too. I'm to get four dollars a week."

"I think she would rather have your companionship than a part of your salary, Clorinda," said Aunt Emmy. "But of course you must decide for yourself, dear. It is hard to be poor. I know it. I am poor."

"You poor!" said Clorinda, kissing her. "Why, you are the richest woman I know, Aunt Emmy – rich in love and goodness and contentment."

"And so are you, dearie . . . rich in youth and health and happiness and ambition. Aren't they all worth while?"

"Of course they are," laughed Clorinda. "Only, unfortunately, Christmas gifts can't be coined out of them."

"Did you ever try?" asked Aunt Emmy. "Think out that question, too, in your thinking out, Clorinda."

"Well, I must say bye-bye and run home. I feel cheered up – you always cheer people up, Aunt Emmy. How grey it is outdoors. I do hope we'll have snow soon. Wouldn't it be jolly to have a white Christmas? We always have such faded brown Decembers."

Clorinda lived just across the road from Aunt Emmy in a tiny white house behind some huge willows. But Aunt Mary lived there too – the only relative Clorinda had, for Aunt Emmy wasn't really her aunt at all. Clorinda had always lived with Aunt Mary ever since she could remember.

Clorinda went home and upstairs to her little room under the eaves, where the great bare willow boughs were branching athwart her windows. She was thinking over what Aunt Emmy had said about Christmas gifts and giving.

"I'm sure I don't know what she could have meant," pondered Clorinda. "I do wish I could find out if it would help me any. I'd love to remember a few of my friends at least. There's Miss Mitchell . . . she's been so good to me all this year and helped me so much with my studies. And there's Mrs. Martin out in Manitoba. If I could only send her something! She must be so lonely out there. And Aunt Emmy herself, of course; and poor old Aunt Kitty down the lane; and Aunt Mary and, yes – Florence too, although she did treat me so meanly. I shall never feel the same to her again. But she gave me a present last Christmas, and so out of mere politeness I ought to give her something."

Clorinda stopped short suddenly. She had just remembered that she would not have liked to say that last sentence to Aunt Emmy. Therefore, there was something wrong about it. Clorinda had long ago learned that there was sure to be something wrong in anything that could not be said to Aunt Emmy. So she stopped to think it over.

Clorinda puzzled over Aunt Emmy's meaning for four days and part of three nights. Then all at once it came to her. Or if it wasn't Aunt Emmy's meaning it was a very good meaning in itself, and it grew clearer and expanded in meaning during the days that followed, although at first Clorinda shrank a little from some of the conclusions to which it led her.

"I've solved the problem of my Christmas giving for this year," she told Aunt Emmy. "I have some things to give after all. Some of them quite costly, too; that is, they will cost me something, but I know I'll be better off and richer after I've paid the price. That is what Mr. Grierson would call a paradox, isn't it? I'll explain all about it to you on Christmas Day."

On Christmas Day, Clorinda went over to Aunt Emmy's. It was a faded brown Christmas after all, for the snow had not come. But Clorinda did not mind; there was such joy in her heart that she thought it the most delightful Christmas Day that ever dawned.

She put the queer cornery armful she carried down on the kitchen floor before she went into the sitting room. Aunt Emmy was lying on the sofa before the fire, and Clorinda sat down beside her.

"I've come to tell you all about it," she said.

Aunt Emmy patted the hand that was in her own.

"From your face, dear girl, it will be pleasant hearing and telling," she said.

Clorinda nodded.

"Aunt Emmy, I thought for days over your meaning . . . thought until I was dizzy. And then one evening it just came to me, without any think-ing at all, and I knew that I could give some gifts after all. I thought of something new every day for a week. At first I didn't think I *could* give some of them, and then I thought how selfish I was. I would have been willing to pay any amount of money for gifts if I had had it, but I wasn't willing to pay what I had. I got over that, though, Aunt Emmy. Now I'm going to tell you what I did give.

"First, there was my teacher, Miss Mitchell. I gave her one of father's books. I have so many of his, you know, so that I wouldn't miss one; but still it was one I loved very much, and so I felt that that love made it worth while. That is, I felt that on second thought. At first, Aunt Emmy, I thought I would be ashamed to offer Miss Mitchell a shabby old book, worn with much reading and all marked over with father's notes and pencillings. I was afraid she would think it queer of me to give her such a present. And yet somehow it seemed to me that it was better than something brand new and unmellowed – that old book which father had loved and which I loved. So I gave it to her, and she understood. I think it pleased her so much, the real meaning in it. She said it was like being given something out of another's heart and life.

"Then you know Mrs. Martin . . . last year she was Miss Hope, my dear Sunday School teacher. She married a home missionary, and they are in a lonely part of the west. Well, I wrote her a letter. Not just an ordinary letter; dear me, no. I took a whole day to write it, and you should have seen the postmistress's eyes stick out when I mailed it. I just told her everything that had happened in Greenvale since she went away. I made it as newsy and cheerful and loving as I possibly could. Everything bright and funny I could think of went into it.

"The next was old Aunt Kitty. You know she was my nurse when I was a baby, and she's very fond of me. But, well, you know, Aunt Emmy, I'm

ashamed to confess it, but really I've never found
Aunt Kitty very entertaining, to put it mildly. She
is always glad when I go to see her, but I've never
gone except when I couldn't help it. She is very
deaf, and rather dull and stupid, you know. Well, I
gave her a whole day. I took my knitting yesterday, and sat with her the whole time and just talked
and talked. I told her all the Greenvale news and
gossip and everything else I thought she'd like to
hear. She was so pleased and proud; she told me
when I came away that she hadn't had such a nice
time for years.

"Then there was . . . Florence. You know, Aunt
Emmy, we were always intimate friends until last
year. Then Florence once told Rose Watson something I had told her in confidence. I found it out
and I was so hurt. I couldn't forgive Florence, and I
told her plainly I could never be a real friend to her
again. Florence felt badly, because she really did love
me, and she asked me to forgive her, but it seemed
as if I couldn't. Well, Aunt Emmy, that was my
Christmas gift to her . . . my forgiveness. I went
down last night and just put my arms around her
and told her that I loved her as much as ever and
wanted to be real close friends again.

"I gave Aunt Mary her gift this morning. I told
her I wasn't going to Murraybridge, that I just

meant to stay home with her. She was so glad – and I'm glad, too, now that I've decided so."

"Your gifts have been real gifts, Clorinda," said Aunt Emmy. "Something of you – the best of you – went into each of them."

Clorinda went out and brought her cornery armful in.

"I didn't forget you, Aunt Emmy," she said, as she unpinned the paper.

There was a rosebush – Clorinda's own pet rosebush – all snowed over with fragrant blossoms.

Aunt Emmy loved flowers. She put her finger under one of the roses and kissed it.

"It's as sweet as yourself, dear child," she said tenderly. "And it will be a joy to me all through the lonely winter days. You've found out the best meaning of Christmas giving, haven't you, dear?"

"Yes, thanks to you, Aunt Emmy," said Clorinda softly.

KATHERINE BROOKE COMES
TO GREEN GABLES

The old porch thermometer says it's zero and the new sidedoor one says it's ten above," remarked Anne, one frosty December night. "So I don't know whether to take my muff or not."

"Better go by the old thermometer," said Rebecca Dew cautiously. "It's probably more used to our climate. Where are you going this cold night, anyway?"

"I'm going round to Temple Street to ask Katherine Brooke to spend the Christmas holidays with me at Green Gables."

"You'll spoil your holidays, then," said Rebecca Dew solemnly. "She'd go about snubbing the angels, that one . . . that is, if she ever condescended to enter heaven. And the worst of it is, she's proud of her bad manners . . . thinks it shows her strength of mind no doubt!"

"My brain agrees with every word you say but my heart simply won't," said Anne. "I feel, in spite of everything, that Katherine Brooke is only a shy, unhappy girl under her disagreeable rind. I can never make any headway with her in Summerside, but if I can get her to Green Gables I believe it will thaw her out."

"You won't get her. She won't go," predicted Rebecca Dew. "Probably she'll take it as an insult to be asked . . . think you're offering her charity. *We* asked her here once to Christmas dinner . . . the year afore you came . . . you remember, Mrs. Mac-Comber, the year we had two turkeys give us and didn't know how we was to get 'em et . . . and all she said was, 'No, thank you. If there's anything I hate, it's the word Christmas!' "

"But that is so dreadful . . . hating Christmas! Something *has* to be done, Rebecca Dew. I'm going to ask her and I've a queer feeling in my thumbs that tells me she will come."

"Somehow," said Rebecca Dew reluctantly, "when you say a thing is going to happen, a body believes it will. You haven't got a second sight, have you? Captain MacComber's mother had it. Useter give me the creeps."

"I don't think I have anything that need give you

creeps. It's only just . . . I've had a feeling for some time that Katherine Brooke is almost crazy with loneliness under her bitter outside and that my invitation will come pat to the psychological moment, Rebecca Dew."

"I am not a B.A.," said Rebecca with awful humility, "and I do not deny your right to use words I cannot always understand. Neither do I deny that you can wind people round your little finger. Look how you managed the Pringles. But I do say I pity you if you take that iceberg and nutmeg grater combined home with you for Christmas."

Anne was by no means as confident as she pretended to be during her walk to Temple Street. Katherine Brooke had really been unbearable of late. Again and again Anne, rebuffed, had said, as grimly as Poe's raven, "Nevermore." Only yesterday Katherine had been positively insulting at a staff meeting. But in an unguarded moment Anne had seen something looking out of the older girl's eyes . . . a passionate, half-frantic something like a caged creature mad with discontent. Anne spent the first half of the night trying to decide whether to invite Katherine Brooke to Green Gables or not. Finally she fell asleep with her mind irrevocably made up.

Katherine's landlady showed Anne into the

parlour and shrugged a fat shoulder when she asked for Miss Brooke.

"I'll tell her you're here but I dunno if she'll come down. She's sulking. I told her at dinner tonight that Mrs. Rawlins says it's scandalous the way she dresses, for a teacher in Summerside High, and she took it high and mighty as usual."

"I don't think you should have told Miss Brooke that," said Anne reproachfully.

"But I thought she ought to know," said Mrs. Dennis somewhat waspishly.

"Did you also think she ought to know that the Inspector said she was one of the best teachers in the Maritimes?" asked Anne. "Or didn't you know it?"

"Oh, I heard it. But she's stuck-up enough now without making her any worse. Proud's no name for it . . . though what she's got to be proud of, *I* dunno. Of course she was mad anyhow tonight because I'd said she couldn't have a dog. She's took a notion into her head she'd like to have a dog. Said she'd pay for his rations and see he was no bother. But what'd I do with him when she was in school? I put my foot down. 'I'm boarding no dogs,' sez I."

"Oh, Mrs. Dennis, won't you let her have a dog? He wouldn't bother you . . . much. You could keep him in the basement while she was in school. And a dog really is such a protection at night. I wish you would . . . *please*."

There was always something about Anne Shirley's eyes when she said "please" that people found hard to resist. Mrs. Dennis, in spite of fat shoulders and a meddlesome tongue, was not unkind at heart. Katherine Brooke simply got under her skin at times with her ungracious ways.

"I dunno why you should worry as to her having a dog or not. I didn't know you were such friends. She hasn't *any* friends. I never had such an unsociable boarder."

"I think that is why she wants a dog, Mrs. Dennis. None of us can live without some kind of companionship."

"Well, it's the first human thing I've noticed about her," said Mrs. Dennis. "I dunno's I have any awful objection to a dog, but she sort of vexed me with her sarcastic way of asking . . . 'I s'pose you wouldn't consent if I asked you if I might have a dog, Mrs. Dennis,' she sez, haughty like. Set her up with it! 'You're s'posing right,' sez I, as haughty as herself. I don't like eating my words any more than most people, but you can tell her she can have a dog if she'll guarantee he won't misbehave in the parlour."

Anne did not think the parlour could be much

worse if the dog did misbehave. She eyed the dingy
lace curtains and the hideous purple roses on the
carpet with a shiver.

"I'm sorry for anyone who has to spend Christmas in a boarding-house like this," she thought. "I
don't wonder Katherine hates the word. I'd like to
give this place a good airing . . . it smells of a thousand meals. *Why* does Katherine go on boarding
here when she has a good salary?"

"She says you can come up," was the message
Mrs. Dennis brought back, rather dubiously, for
Miss Brooke had run true to form.

The narrow, steep stair was repellent. It didn't
want you. Nobody would go up who didn't have
to. The linoleum in the hall was worn to shreds.
The little back hall-bedroom where Anne presently
found herself was even more cheerless than the
parlour. It was lighted by one glaring unshaded gas
jet. There was an iron bed with a valley in the
middle of it and a narrow, sparsely draped window
looking out on a backyard garden where a large
crop of tin cans flourished. But beyond it was a
marvellous sky and a row of lombardies standing
out against long, purple, distant hills.

"Oh, Miss Brooke, look at that sunset," said
Anne rapturously from the squeaky, cushionless
rocker to which Katherine had ungraciously
pointed her.

"I've seen a good many sunsets," said the latter coldly, without moving. ("Condescending to me with your sunsets!" she thought bitterly.)

"You haven't seen this one. No two sunsets are alike. Just sit down here and let us let it sink into our souls," *said* Anne. *Thought* Anne, "Do you *ever* say anything pleasant?"

"Don't be ridiculous, please."

The most insulting words in the world! With an added edge of insult in Katherine's contemptuous tones. Anne turned from her sunset and looked at Katherine, much more than half inclined to get up and walk out. But Katherine's eyes looked a trifle strange. *Had* she been crying? Surely not . . . you couldn't imagine Katherine Brooke crying.

"You don't make me feel very welcome," Anne said slowly.

"I can't pretend things. I haven't *your* notable gift for doing the queen act . . . saying exactly the right thing to every one. You're *not* welcome. What sort of room is this to welcome anyone to?"

Katherine made a scornful gesture at the faded walls, the shabby bare chairs and the wobbly dressing-table with its petticoat of limp muslin.

"It isn't a nice room, but why do you stay here if you don't like it?"

"Oh . . . why . . . Why? *You* wouldn't understand.

It doesn't matter. I don't care what anybody thinks. What brought you here tonight? I don't suppose you came just to soak in the sunset."

"I came to ask if you would spend the Christmas holidays with me at Green Gables."

("Now," thought Anne, "for another broadside of sarcasm! I do wish she'd sit down at least. She just stands there as if waiting for me to go.")

But there was silence for a moment. Then Katherine said slowly,

"Why do you ask me? It isn't because you like me . . . even you couldn't pretend *that*."

"It's because I can't bear to think of any human being spending Christmas in a place like *this*," said Anne candidly.

The sarcasm came then.

"Oh, I see. A seasonable outburst of charity. I'm hardly a candidate for that *yet*, Miss Shirley."

Anne got up. She was out of patience with this strange, aloof creature. She walked across the room and looked Katherine squarely in the eye. "Katherine Brooke, whether you know it or not, what *you* want is a good spanking."

They gazed at each other for a moment.

"It must have relieved you to say that," said Katherine. But somehow the insulting tone had gone out of her voice. There was even a faint twitch at the corner of her mouth.

"It has," said Anne. "I've been wanting to tell you just that for some time. I didn't ask you to Green Gables out of charity . . . you know perfectly well. I told you my true reason. *Nobody* ought to spend Christmas here . . . the very idea is indecent."

"You asked me to Green Gables just because you are sorry for me."

"I *am* sorry for you. Because you've shut out life . . . and now life is shutting you out. Stop it, Katherine. Open your doors to life . . . and life will come in."

"The Anne Shirley version of the old bromide, 'If you bring a smiling visage to the glass you meet a smile,'" said Katherine with a shrug.

"Like all bromides, that's absolutely true. Now, are you coming to Green Gables or are you not?"

"What would you say if I accepted . . . to yourself, not to me?"

"I'd say you were showing the first faint glimmer of common sense I'd ever detected in you," retorted Anne.

Katherine laughed . . . surprisingly. She walked across to the window, scowled at the fiery streak which was all that was left of the scorned sunset, and then turned.

"Very well . . . I'll go. Now you can go through the motions of telling me you're delighted and that we'll have a jolly time."

"I *am* delighted. But I don't know if you'll have a jolly time or not. That will depend a good deal on yourself, Miss Brooke."

"Oh, I'll behave myself decently. You'll be surprised. You won't find me a very exhilarating guest, I suppose, but I promise you I won't eat with my knife or insult people when they tell me it's a fine day. I tell you frankly that the only reason I'm going is because even I can't stick the thought of spending the holidays here alone. Mrs. Dennis is going to spend Christmas week with her daughter in Charlottetown. It's a bore to think of getting my own meals. I'm a rotten cook. So much for the triumph of matter over mind. But will you give me your word of honour that you won't wish me a merry Christmas? I just don't want to be merry at Christmas."

"I won't. But I can't answer for the twins."

"I'm not going to ask you to sit down here . . . you'd freeze . . . but I see that there's a very fine moon in place of your sunset and I'll walk home with you and help you to admire it if you like."

"I do like," said Anne, "but I want to impress on your mind that we have *much* finer moons in Avonlea."

"So she's going?" said Rebecca Dew as she filled Anne's hot-water bottle. "Well, Miss Shirley, I hope you'll never try to induce me to turn

Mohammedan . . . because you'd likely succeed. Where *is* That Cat? Out frisking round Summerside and the weather at zero."

"Not by the new thermometer. And Dusty Miller is curled up on the rocking-chair by my stove in the tower, snoring with happiness."

"Ah well," said Rebecca Dew with a little shiver as she shut the kitchen door, "I wish every one in the world was as warm and sheltered as we are tonight." . . .

ANNE WAS ALREADY tasting Christmas happiness. She fairly sparkled as the train left the station. The ugly streets slipped past her . . . she was going home . . . home to Green Gables. Out in the open country the world was all golden-white and pale violet, woven here and there with the dark magic of spruces and the leafless delicacy of birches. The low sun behind the bare woods seemed rushing through the trees like a splendid god, as the train sped on. Katherine was silent but did not seem ungracious.

"Don't expect me to talk," she had warned Anne curtly.

"I won't. I hope you don't think I'm one of those terrible people who make you feel that you *have* to talk to them all the time. We'll just talk when we feel like it. I admit I'm likely to feel like it a good part of the time, but you're under no obligation to take any notice of what I'm saying."

Davy met them at Bright River with a big two-seated sleigh full of furry robes . . . and a bear hug for Anne. The two girls snuggled down in the back seat. The drive from the station to Green Gables had always been a very pleasant part of Anne's weekends home. She always recalled her first drive home from Bright River with Matthew. That had been in spring and this was December, but everything along the road kept saying to her, "Do you remember?" The snow crisped under the runners; the music of the bells tinkled through the ranks of tall pointed firs, snow-laden. The White Way of Delight had little festoons of stars tangled in the trees. And on the last hill but one they saw the great gulf, white and mystical under the moon but not yet ice-bound.

"There's just one spot on this road where I always feel suddenly . . . 'I'm *home*,'" said Anne. "It's the top of the next hill, where we'll see the lights of Green Gables. I'm just thinking of the supper Marilla will have ready for us. I believe I can smell it here. Oh, it's good . . . good . . . good to be home again!"

At Green Gables every tree in the yard seemed to welcome her back . . . every lighted window was beckoning. And how good Marilla's kitchen smelled as they opened the door. There were hugs and exclamations and laughter. Even Katherine seemed somehow no outsider, but one of them. Mrs. Rachel Lynde had set her cherished parlour lamp on the supper-table and lighted it. It was really a hideous thing with a hideous red globe, but what a warm rosy becoming light it cast over everything! How warm and friendly were the shadows! How pretty Dora was growing! And Davy really seemed almost a man.

There was news to tell. Diana had a small daughter . . . Josie Pye actually had a young man . . . and Charlie Sloane was said to be engaged. It was all just as exciting as news of empire could have been. Mrs. Lynde's new patchwork quilt, just completed, containing five thousand pieces, was on display and received its meed of praise.

"When you come home, Anne," said Davy, "everything seems to come alive."

"Ah, this is how life should be," purred Dora's kitten.

"I've always found it hard to resist the lure of a moonlight night," said Anne after supper. "How about a snow-shoe tramp, Miss Brooke? I think that I've heard that you snow-shoe."

"Yes . . . it's the only thing I *can* do . . . but I haven't done it for six years," said Katherine with a shrug.

Anne rooted out her snow-shoes from the garret and Davy shot over to Orchard Slope to borrow an old pair of Diana's for Katherine. They went through Lover's Lane, full of lovely tree shadows, and across fields where little fir trees fringed the fences and through woods which were full of secrets they seemed always on the point of whispering to you but never did . . . and through open glades that were like pools of silver.

They did not talk or want to talk. It was as if they were afraid to talk for fear of spoiling something beautiful. But Anne had never felt so *near* Katherine Brooke before. By some magic of its own the winter night had brought them together . . . *almost* together but not quite.

When they came out to the main road and a sleigh flashed by, bells ringing, laughter tinkling, both girls gave an involuntary sigh. It seemed to both that they were leaving behind a world that had nothing in common with the one to which they were returning . . . a world where time was not . . . which was young with immortal youth . . . where souls communed with each other in some medium that needed nothing so crude as words.

"It's been wonderful," said Katherine so obviously to herself that Anne made no response.

They went down the road and up the long Green Gables land but just before they reached the yard gate, they both paused as by a common impulse and stood in silence, leaning against the old mossy fence, and looked at the brooding motherly old house seen dimly through its veil of trees. How beautiful Green Gables was on a winter night!

Below it the Lake of Shining Waters was locked in ice, patterned around its edges with tree shadows. Silence was everywhere, save for the staccato clip of a horse trotting over the bridge. Anne smiled to recall how often she had heard that sound as she lay in her gable room and pretended to herself that it was the gallop of fairy horses passing in the night.

Suddenly another sound broke the stillness.

"Katherine . . . you're . . . why, you're not crying!"

Somehow, it seemed impossible to think of Katherine crying. But she was. And her tears suddenly humanized her. Anne no longer felt afraid of her.

"Katherine . . . dear Katherine . . . what is the matter? Can I help?"

"Oh . . . you can't understand!" gasped Katherine. "Things have always been made easy for *you*. You . . . you seem to live in a little enchanted circle of beauty and romance. 'I wonder what delightful discovery I'll make today' . . . that seems to be your attitude to life, Anne. As for me, I've forgotten how to live . . . no, I never knew how. I'm . . . I'm like a creature caught in a trap. I can never get out . . . and it seems to me that somebody is always poking sticks at me through the bars. And you . . . you have more happiness than you know what to do with . . . friends everywhere, a lover! Not that I want a lover . . . I hate men . . . but if I died tonight, not one living soul would miss me. How would you like to be absolutely friendless in the world?"

Katherine's voice broke in another sob.

"Katherine, you say you like frankness. I'm going to be frank. If you are as friendless as you say, it is your own fault. I've wanted to be friends with you. But you've been all prickles and stings."

"Oh, I know . . . I know. How I hated you when you came first! Flaunting your circlet of pearls . . . "

"Katherine, I didn't 'flaunt' it!"

"Oh, I suppose not. That's just my natural hatefulness. But it seemed to flaunt itself . . . not that I envied you your beau . . . I've never wanted to be married . . . I saw enough of *that* with Father and Mother . . . but I hated your being over me when you were younger than I . . . I was glad when the Pringles made trouble for you. You seemed to have everything I hadn't . . . charm . . . friendship . . . youth. Youth! I never had anything but starved youth. You know nothing about it. You don't know . . . you haven't the least idea what it is like not to be wanted by anyone . . . anyone!"

"Oh, haven't I?" cried Anne.

In a few poignant sentences she sketched her childhood before coming to Green Gables.

"I wish I'd known that," said Katherine. "It would have made a difference. To me you seemed one of the favourites of fortune. I've been eating my heart out with envy of you. You got the position I wanted . . . oh, I know you're better qualified than I am, but there it was. You're pretty . . . at least you make people believe you're pretty. *My* earliest recollection is of someone saying, 'What an ugly child!' You come into a room delightfully . . . oh, I remember how you came into school that first morning. But I think the real reason I've hated you so is that you always seemed to have some secret delight . . . as if every day of life was an adventure. In spite of my hatred there were times when I acknowledged to myself that you might just have come from some far-off star."

"Really, Katherine, you take my breath with all these compliments. But you don't hate me any longer, do you? We can be friends now."

"I don't know . . . I've never had a friend of any kind, much less one of anything like my own age. I don't belong anywhere . . . never have belonged. I don't think I know how to *be* a friend. No, I don't hate you any longer . . . I don't know how I feel about you . . . oh, I suppose it's your noted charm beginning to work on me. I only know that I feel I'd like to tell you what my life has been like. I could never have told you if you hadn't told me about your life before you came to Green Gables. I want you to understand what has made me as I am. I don't know why I should want you to understand . . . but I do."

"Tell me, Katherine dear. I do want to understand you."

"You *do* know what it is like not to be wanted, I admit . . . but not what it is like to know that your father and mother don't want you. Mine didn't. They hated me from the moment I was born . . . and before . . . and they hated each other. Yes, they did. They quarrelled continually . . . just mean, nagging, petty quarrels. My childhood was a nightmare. They died when I was seven and I went to live with Uncle Henry's family. *They* didn't want me either. They all looked down on me because I was 'living on their charity.' I remember all the snubs I got . . . every one. I can't remember a single kind word. I had to wear my cousins' cast-off clothes. I remember one hat in particular . . . it made me look like a mushroom. And they made fun of me whenever I put it on. One day I tore it off and threw it on the fire. I had to wear the most awful old tam to church all the rest of the winter. I never even had a dog . . . and I wanted one so. I had some brains ... I longed so for a B.A. course ... but naturally I might just as well have yearned for the moon. However, Uncle Henry agreed to put me through Queen's if I would pay him back when I got a school. He paid my board in a miserable third-rate boarding-house where I had a room over the kitchen that was ice cold in winter and boiling hot in summer, and full of stale cooking smells in all seasons. And the clothes I had to wear to Queen's! But I got my licence and I got the second room in Summerside High ... the only bit of luck I've ever had. Ever since then I've been pinching and scrimping to pay Uncle Henry ... not only what he spent putting me through Queen's, but what my board through all the years I lived there cost him. I was determined I would not owe him one cent. That is why I've boarded with Mrs. Dennis and dressed shabbily. And I've just finished paying him. For the first time in my life I feel *free*. But meanwhile I've developed the wrong way. I know I'm unsocial ... I know I can never think of the right thing to say. I know it's my own fault that I'm always neglected and overlooked at social functions. I know I've made being disagreeable into a fine art. I know I'm sarcastic. I know I'm regarded as a tyrant by my pupils. I know they hate me. Do you think it doesn't hurt me to know it? They always look afraid of me ... I hate people who look as if they were afraid of me. Oh, Anne, hate's got to be a disease with me. I do want to be like other people . . . and I never can now. *That* is what makes me so bitter."

"Oh, but you can!" Anne put her arm about Katherine. "You can put hate out of your mind . . . cure yourself of it. Life is only beginning for you now . . . since at last you're quite free and independent. And you never know what may be around the next bend in the road."

"I've heard you say that before . . . I've laughed at your 'bend in the road.' But the trouble is there aren't any bends in my road. I can see it stretching straight out before me to the sky-line . . . endless monotony. Oh, does life ever *frighten* you, Anne, with its *blankness* . . . its swarms of cold, uninteresting people? No, of course it doesn't. *You* don't have to go on teaching all the rest of your life. And you seem to find *everybody* interesting, even that little round red being you call Rebecca Dew. The truth is, I hate teaching . . . and there's nothing else I can do. A schoolteacher is simply a slave of time. Oh, I know you like it . . . I don't see how you can. Anne, I want to travel. It's the one thing I've always longed for. I remember the one and only picture that hung on the wall of my attic room at Uncle Henry's . . . a faded old print that had been discarded from the other rooms with scorn. It was a picture of palms around a spring in the desert, with a string of camels marching away in the distance. It literally fascinated me. I've always wanted to go and find it . . . I want to see the Southern Cross and the Taj Mahal and the pillars of Karnak. I want to *know* . . . not just *believe* . . . that the world is round. And I can never do it on a teacher's salary. I'll just have to go on forever, prating of King Henry the Eighth's wives and the inexhaustible resources of the Dominion."

Anne laughed. It was safe to laugh now, for the bitterness had gone out of Katherine's voice. It sounded merely rueful and impatient.

"Anyhow, we're going to be friends . . . and we're going to have a jolly ten days here to begin our friendship. I've always wanted to be friends with you, Katherine . . . spelled with a K! I've always felt that underneath all your prickles was something that would make you worth while as a friend."

"So that is what you've really thought of me? I've often wondered. Well, the leopard will have a go at changing its spots if it's at all possible. Perhaps it is. I can believe almost anything at this Green Gables of yours. It's the first place I've ever been in that felt like a *home*. I should like to be more like other people . . . if it isn't too late. I'll even

practise a sunny smile for that Gilbert of yours
when he arrives tomorrow night. Of course I've
forgotten how to talk to young men . . . if I ever
knew. He'll just think me an old-maid gooseberry.
I wonder if, when I go to bed tonight, I'll feel
furious with myself for pulling off my mask and
letting you see into my shivering soul like this."

"No, you won't. You'll think, 'I'm glad she's
found out I'm human.' We're going to snuggle
down among the warm fluffy blankets, probably
with two hot-water bottles, for likely Marilla and
Mrs. Lynde will each put one in for us for fear the
other has forgotten it. And you'll feel deliciously
sleepy after this walk in the frosty moonshine . . .
and first thing you'll know, it will be morning and
you'll feel as if you were the first person to discover
that the sky is blue. And you'll grow learned in lore
of plum puddings because you're going to help me
make one for Tuesday . . . a great big plummy one."

Anne was amazed at Katherine's good looks
when they went in. Her complexion was radiant
after her long walk in the keen air and colour made
all the difference in the world to her.

"Why, Katherine would be handsome if she
wore the right kind of hats and dresses," reflected
Anne, trying to imagine Katherine with a certain
dark, richly red velvet hat she had seen in a

Summerside shop, on her black hair and pulled over her amber eyes. "I've simply got to see what can be done about it."

SATURDAY AND MONDAY were full of gay doings at Green Gables. The plum pudding was concocted and the Christmas tree brought home. Katherine and Anne and Davy and Dora went to the woods for it . . . a beautiful little fir to whose cutting down Anne was only reconciled by the fact that it was in a little clearing of Mr. Harrison's which was going to be stumped and ploughed in the spring anyhow.

They wandered about, gathering creeping spruce and ground pine for wreaths . . . even some ferns that kept green in a certain deep hollow of the woods all winter . . . until day smiled back at night over white-bosomed hills and they came back to Green Gables in triumph . . . to meet a tall young man with hazel eyes and the beginnings of a moustache which made him look so much older and maturer that Anne had one awful moment of wondering if it were really Gilbert or a stranger.

Katherine, with a little smile that tried to be sarcastic but couldn't quite succeed, left them in the parlour and played games with the twins in the kitchen all the evening. To her amazement she found she was enjoying it. And what fun it was to go down cellar with Davy and find that there were really such things as sweet apples still left in the world.

Katherine had never been in a country cellar before and had no idea what a delightful, spooky, shadowy place it could be by candle-light. Life already seemed *warmer*. For the first time it came home to Katherine that life might be beautiful, even for her.

Davy made enough noise to wake the Seven Sleepers at an unearthly hour Christmas morning, ringing an old cow-bell up and down the stairs. Marilla was horrified at his doing such a thing when there was a guest in the house, but Katherine came down laughing. Somehow, an odd camaraderie had sprung up between her and Davy. She told Anne candidly that she had no use for the impeccable Dora but that Davy was somehow tarred with her own brush.

They opened the parlour and distributed the gifts before breakfast because the twins, even Dora, couldn't have eaten anything if they hadn't. Katherine, who had not expected anything except, perhaps, a duty gift from Anne, found herself getting presents from everyone. A gay, crocheted afghan from Mrs. Lynde . . . a sachet of orris root from Dora . . . a paper-knife from Davy . . . a basketful of tiny jars of jam and jelly from Marilla . . .

even a little bronze chessy cat for a paper-weight from Gilbert.

And, tied under the tree, curled up on a bit of warm and woolly blanket, a dear little brown-eyed puppy, with alert, silken ears and an ingratiating tail. A card tied to his neck bore the legend, "From Anne, who dares, after all, to wish you a Merry Christmas."

Katherine gathered his wriggling little body up in her arms and spoke shakily.

"Anne . . . he's a darling! But Mrs. Dennis won't let me keep him. I asked her if I might get a dog and she refused."

"I've arranged it all with Mrs. Dennis. You'll find she won't object. And, anyway, Katherine, you're not going to be there long. You *must* find a decent place to live, now that you've paid off what you thought were your obligations. Look at the lovely box of stationery Diana sent me. Isn't it fascinating to look at the blank pages and wonder what will be written on them?"

Mrs. Lynde was thankful it was a white Christmas . . . there would be no fat graveyards when Christmas was white . . . but to Katherine it seemed a purple and crimson and golden Christmas. And the week that followed was just as beautiful. Katherine had often wondered bitterly just what it would be like to be happy and now she found out. She bloomed out in the most astonishing way. Anne found herself enjoying their companionship.

"To think I was afraid she would spoil my Christmas holiday!" she reflected in amazement.

"To think," said Katherine to herself, "that I was on the verge of refusing to come here when Anne invited me!"

They went for long walks . . . through Lover's Lane and the Haunted Wood, where the very silence seemed friendly . . . over hills where the light snow whirled in a winter dance of goblins . . . through old orchards full of violet shadows . . . through the glory of sunset woods. There were no birds to chirp or sing, no brooks to gurgle, no squirrels to gossip. But the wind made occasional music that had in quality what it lacked in quantity.

"One can always find something lovely to look at or listen to," said Anne.

They talked of "cabbages and kings," and hitched their wagons to stars, and came home with appetites that taxed even the Green Gables pantry. One day it stormed and they couldn't go out. The east wind was beating around the eaves and the grey gulf was roaring. But even a storm at Green Gables had charms of its own. It was cosy to sit by the stove and dreamily watch the firelight flickering over the ceiling while you munched apples and candy. How jolly supper was with the storm wailing outside!

One night Gilbert took them to see Diana and her new baby daughter.

"I never held a baby in my life before," said Katherine as they drove home. "For one thing, I didn't want to, and for another I'd have been afraid of it going to pieces in my grasp. You can't imagine how I felt . . . so big and clumsy with that tiny, exquisite thing in my arms. I know Mrs. Wright thought I was going to drop it every minute. I could see her striving heroically to conceal her terror. But it did something to me . . . the baby I mean . . . I haven't decided just what."

"Babies are such fascinating creatures," said Anne dreamily. "They are what I heard somebody at Redmond call, 'terrific bundles of potentialities.' Think of it, Katherine . . . Homer must have been a baby once . . . a baby with dimples and great eyes full of light . . . he couldn't have been blind then, of course."

"What a pity his mother didn't know he was to be Homer," said Katherine.

"But I think I'm glad Judas's mother didn't know he was to be Judas," said Anne softly. "I hope she never did know."

THERE WAS A CONCERT in the hall one night, with a party at Abner Sloane's after it, and Anne persuaded Katherine to go to both.

"I want you to give us a reading for our program, Katherine. I've heard you read beautifully."

"I used to recite . . . I think I rather liked doing it. But the summer before last I recited at a shore concert which a party of summer resorters got up . . . and I heard them laughing at me afterwards."

"How do you know they were laughing at you?"

"They must have been. There wasn't anything else to laugh at."

Anne hid a smile and persisted in asking for the reading.

"Give *Genevra* for an encore. I'm told you do that splendidly. Mrs. Stephen Pringle told me she never slept a wink that night after she heard you give it."

"No; I've never liked *Genevra*. It's in the reading, so I try occasionally to show the class how to read it. I really have no patience with Genevra. Why didn't she scream when she found herself locked in? When they were hunting everywhere for her, surely somebody would have heard her."

Katherine finally promised the reading but was dubious about the party. "I'll go, of course. But nobody will ask me to dance and I'll feel sarcastic and prejudiced and ashamed. I'm always miserable at parties . . . the few I've ever gone to. Nobody seems to think I can dance . . . and you know I can fairly well, Anne. I picked it up at Uncle Henry's, because a poor bit of a maid they had wanted to learn too, and she and I used to dance together in the kitchen at night to the music that went on in the parlour. I think I'd like it . . . with the right kind of partner."

"You won't be miserable at this party, Katherine. You won't be outside looking in. There's all the difference in the world, you know, between being inside looking out and outside looking in. You have such lovely hair, Katherine. Do you mind if I try a new way of doing it?"

Katherine shrugged.

"Oh, go ahead. I suppose my hair does look dreadful . . . but I've no time to be always primping. I haven't a party dress. Will my green taffeta do?"

"It will have to do . . . though green is the one colour above all others that you should never wear, my Katherine. But you're going to wear a red, pintucked chiffon collar I've made for you. Yes, you *are*. You ought to have a red dress, Katherine."

"I've always hated red. When I went to live with Uncle Henry, Aunt Gertrude always made me wear aprons of bright Turkey-red. The other children in school used to call out 'Fire,' when I came in with one of those aprons on. Anyway, I can't be bothered with clothes."

"Heaven grant me patience! Clothes are *very* important," said Anne severely, as she braided and coiled. Then she looked at her work and saw that it was good. She put her arm about Katherine's shoulders and turned her to the mirror.

"Don't you truly think we are a pair of quite good-looking girls?" she laughed. "And isn't it really nice to think people will find some pleasure in looking at us? There are so many homely people who would actually look quite attractive if they took a little pains with themselves. Three Sundays ago in church . . . you remember the day poor old Mr. Milvain preached and had such a terrible cold in his head that nobody could make out what he was saying? . . . well, I passed the time making the people around me beautiful. I gave Mrs. Brent a new nose, I waved Mary Addison's hair and gave Jane Marden's a lemon rinse . . . I dressed Emma Dill in blue instead of brown . . . I dressed Charlotte Blair in stripes instead of checks . . . I removed several moles . . . and I shaved off Thomas Anderson's long, sandy Piccadilly weepers. You couldn't have known them when I got through with them. And, except perhaps for Mrs. Brent's nose, they could have done everything I did, themselves. Why, Katherine, your eyes are just the colour of tea . . . amber tea. Now, live up to your name this evening . . . a brook should be sparkling . . . limpid . . . merry."

"Everything I'm not."

"Everything you've been this past week. So you *can* be it."

"That's only the magic of Green Gables. When I go back to Summerside, twelve o'clock will have struck for Cinderella."

"You'll take the magic back with you. Look at yourself . . . looking for once as you ought to look all the time."

Katherine gazed at her reflection in the mirror as if rather doubting her identity.

"I do look years younger," she admitted. "You were right . . . clothes *do* do things to you. Oh, I know I've been looking older than my age. I didn't care. Why should I? Nobody else cared. And I'm not like you, Anne. Apparently you were born knowing how to live. And I don't know anything about it . . . not even the A B C. I wonder if it's too late to learn. I've been sarcastic so long, I don't know if I can be anything else. Sarcasm seemed to me to be the only way I could make any impression on people. And it seems to me, too, that I've always been afraid when I was in the company of other people . . . afraid of saying something stupid . . . afraid of being laughed at."

"Katherine Brooke, look at yourself in that mirror; carry that picture of yourself with you . . . magnificent hair framing your face instead of trying to pull it backward . . . eyes sparkling like dark stars . . . a little flush of excitement on your cheeks . . . and you won't feel afraid. Come, now. We're going to be late, but fortunately all the performers have what I heard Dora referring to as 'preserved' seats."

Gilbert drove them to the hall. How like old times it was . . . only Katherine was with her in place of Diana. Anne sighed. Diana had so many other interests now. No more running round to concerts and parties for her.

But what an evening it was! What silvery satin roads with a pale green sky in the west after a light snowfall! Orion was treading his stately march across the heavens, and hills and fields and woods lay around them in a pearly silence.

Katherine's reading captured her audience from the first line, and at the party she could not find dances for all her would-be partners. She suddenly found herself laughing without bitterness. Then home to Green Gables, warming their toes at the sitting-room fire by the light of two friendly candles on the mantel; and Mrs. Lynde tiptoeing into their room, late as it was, to ask them if they'd like another blanket and assure Katherine that her little dog was snug and warm in a basket behind the kitchen stove.

"I've got a new outlook on life," thought Katherine as she drifted off to slumber. "I didn't know there were people like this."

"Come again," said Marilla when she left.

Marilla never said that to anyone unless she meant it. "Of course she's coming again," said Anne. "For weekends . . . and for *weeks* in the summer. We'll build bonfires and hoe in the garden . . . and pick apples and go for the cows . . . and row on the pond and get lost in the woods. I want to show you Little Hester Gray's garden, Katherine, and Echo Lodge and Violet Vale when it's full of violets."

A CHRISTMAS MISTAKE

omorrow is Christmas," announced Teddy Grant exultantly, as he sat on the floor struggling manfully with a refractory boot-lace that was knotted and tagless and stubbornly refused to go into the eyelets of Teddy's patched boots. "Ain't I glad, though. Hurrah!"

His mother was washing the breakfast dishes in a dreary, listless sort of way. She looked tired and broken-spirited. Ted's enthusiasm seemed to grate on her, for she answered sharply:

"Christmas, indeed. I can't see that it is anything for us to rejoice over. Other people may be glad enough, but what with winter coming on I'd sooner it was spring than Christmas. Mary Alice, do lift that child out of the ashes and put its shoes and stockings on. Everything seems to be at sixes and sevens here this morning."

Keith, the oldest boy, was coiled up on the sofa calmly working out some algebra problems, quite oblivious to the noise around him. But he looked up from his slate, with his pencil suspended above an obstinate equation, to declaim with a flourish:

"Christmas comes but once a year,

And then Mother wishes it wasn't here."

"I don't, then," said Gordon, son number two, who was preparing his own noon lunch of bread and molasses at the table, and making an atrocious mess of crumbs and sugary syrup over everything. "I know one thing to be thankful for, and that is that there'll be no school. We'll have a whole week of holidays."

Gordon was noted for his aversion to school and his affection for holidays.

"And we're going to have turkey for dinner," declared Teddy, getting up off the floor and rushing to secure his share of bread and molasses, "and cranb'ry sauce and – and – pound cake! Ain't we, Ma?"

"No, you are not," said Mrs. Grant desperately, dropping the dishcloth and snatching the baby on her knee to wipe the crust of cinders and molasses from the chubby pink-and-white face. "You may as well know it now, children, I've kept it from you so far in hopes that something would turn up, but nothing has. We can't have any Christmas dinner tomorrow — we can't afford it. I've pinched and saved every way I could for the last month, hoping that I'd be able to get a turkey for you anyhow, but you'll have to do without it. There's that doctor's bill to pay and a dozen other bills coming in — and people say they can't wait. I suppose they can't, but it's kind of hard, I must say."

The little Grants stood with open mouths and horrified eyes. No turkey for Christmas! Was the world coming to an end? Wouldn't the government interfere if anyone ventured to dispense with a Christmas celebration?

The gluttonous Teddy stuffed his fists into his eyes and lifted up his voice. Keith, who understood better than the others the look on his mother's face, took his blubbering young brother by the collar and marched him into the porch. The twins, seeing the summary proceeding, swallowed the outcries they had intended to make, although they couldn't keep a few big tears from running down their fat cheeks.

Mrs. Grant looked pityingly at the disappointed faces about her.

"Don't cry, children, you make me feel worse. We are not the only ones who will have to do without a Christmas turkey. We ought to be very thankful that we have anything to eat at all. I hate to disappoint you, but it can't be helped."

"Never mind, Mother," said Keith, comfortingly,

relaxing his hold upon the porch door, whereupon it suddenly flew open and precipitated Teddy, who had been tugging at the handle, heels over head backwards. "We know you've done your best. It's been a hard year for you. Just wait, though. I'll soon be grown up, and then you and these greedy youngsters shall feast on turkey every day of the year. Hello, Teddy, have you got on your feet again? Mind, sir, no more blubbering!"

"When I'm a man," announced Teddy with dignity, "I'd just like to see you put me in the porch. And I mean to have turkey all the time and I won't give you any, either."

"All right, you greedy small boy. Only take yourself off to school now, and let us hear no more squeaks out of you. Tramp, all of you, and give Mother a chance to get her work done."

Mrs. Grant got up and fell to work at her dishes with a brighter face.

"Well, we mustn't give in; perhaps things will be better after a while. I'll make a famous bread pudding, and you can boil some molasses taffy and ask those little Smithsons next door to help you pull it. They won't whine for turkey, I'll be bound. I don't suppose they ever tasted such a thing in all their lives. If I could afford it, I'd have had them all in to dinner with us. That sermon Mr. Evans preached last Sunday kind of stirred me up. He said we ought always to try and share our Christmas joy with some poor souls who had never learned the meaning of the word. I can't do as much as I'd like to. It was different when your father was alive."

The noisy group grew silent as they always did when their father was spoken of. He had died the year before, and since his death the little family had had a hard time. Keith, to hide his feelings, began to hector the rest.

"Mary Alice, do hurry up. Here, you twin nuisances, get off to school. If you don't you'll be late and then the master will give you a whipping."

"He won't," answered the irrepressible Teddy. "He never whips us, he doesn't. He stands us on the floor sometimes, though," he added, remembering the many times his own chubby legs had been seen to better advantage on the school platform.

"That man," said Mrs. Grant, alluding to the teacher, "makes me nervous. He is the most abstracted creature I ever saw in my life. It is a wonder to me he doesn't walk straight into the river some day. You'll meet him meandering along the street, gazing into vacancy, and he'll never see you nor hear a word you say half the time."

"Yesterday," said Gordon, chuckling over the remembrance, "he came in with a big piece of paper he'd picked up on the entry floor in one hand and his hat in the other – and he stuffed his hat into the coal-scuttle and hung up the paper on a nail as grave as you please. Never knew the difference till Ned Slocum went and told him. He's always doing things like that."

Keith had collected his books and now marched his brothers and sisters off to school. Left alone with the baby, Mrs. Grant betook herself to her work with a heavy heart. But a second interruption broke the progress of her dish-washing.

"I declare," she said, with a surprised glance through the window, "if there isn't that absent-minded schoolteacher coming through the yard! What can he want? Dear me, I do hope Teddy hasn't been cutting capers in school again."

For the teacher's last call had been in October and had been occasioned by the fact that the irre-pressible Teddy would persist in going to school with his pockets filled with live crickets and in driving them harnessed to strings up and down the aisle when the teacher's back was turned. All mild methods of punishment having failed, the teacher had called to talk it over with Mrs. Grant, with the happy result that Teddy's behaviour had improved – in the matter of crickets at least.

But it was about time for another outbreak. Teddy had been unnaturally good for too long a time. Poor Mrs. Grant feared that it was the calm before a storm, and it was with nervous haste that she went to the door and greeted the young teacher.

He was a slight, pale, boyish-looking fellow, with an abstracted, musing look in his large dark eyes. Mrs. Grant noticed with amusement that he wore a white straw hat in spite of the season. His eyes were directed to her face with his usual unseeing gaze.

"Just as though he was looking through me at something a thousand miles away," said Mrs. Grant afterwards. "I believe he was, too. His body was right there on the step before me, but where his soul was is more than you or I or anybody can tell."

"Good morning," he said absently. "I have just called on my way to school with a message from Miss Millar. She wants you all to come up and have Christmas dinner with her tomorrow."

"For the land's sake!" said Mrs. Grant blankly. "I don't understand." To herself she thought, "I wish I dared take him and shake him to find if he's walking in his sleep or not."

"You and all the children – every one," went on the teacher dreamily, as if he were reciting a lesson learned beforehand. "She told me to tell you to be sure and come. Shall I say that you will?"

"Oh, yes, that is – I suppose – I don't know," said

Mrs. Grant incoherently. "I never expected – yes, you may tell her we'll come," she concluded abruptly.

"Thank you," said the abstracted messenger, gravely lifting his hat and looking squarely through Mrs. Grant into unknown regions. When he had gone Mrs. Grant went in and sat down, laughing in a sort of hysterical way.

"I wonder if it is all right. Could Cornelia really have told him? She must, I suppose, but it is enough to take one's breath."

Mrs. Grant and Cornelia Millar were cousins, and had once been the closest of friends, but that was years ago, before some spiteful reports and ill-natured gossip had come between them, making only a little rift at first that soon widened into a chasm of coldness and alienation. Therefore this invitation surprised Mrs. Grant greatly.

Miss Cornelia was a maiden lady of certain years, with a comfortable bank account and a handsome, old-fashioned house on the hill behind the village. She always boarded the schoolteachers and looked after them maternally; she was an active church worker and a tower of strength to struggling ministers and their families.

"If Cornelia has seen fit at last to hold out the hand of reconciliation I'm glad enough to take it. Dear knows, I've wanted to make up often enough, but I didn't think she ever would. We've both of us got too much pride and stubbornness. It's the Turner blood in us that does it. The Turners were all so set. But I mean to do my part now she has done hers."

And Mrs. Grant made a final attack on the dishes with a beaming face.

When the little Grants came home and heard the news, Teddy stood on his head to express his delight, the twins kissed each other, and Mary Alice and Gordon danced around the kitchen.

Keith thought himself too big to betray any joy over a Christmas dinner, but he whistled while doing the chores until the bare welkin in the yard rang, and Teddy, in spite of unheard of misdemeanours, was not collared off into the porch once.

When the young teacher got home from school that evening he found the yellow house full of all sorts of delectable odours. Miss Cornelia herself was concocting mince pies after the famous family recipe, while her ancient and faithful handmaiden, Hannah, was straining into moulds the cranberry jelly. The open pantry door revealed a tempting array of Christmas delicacies.

"Did you call and invite the Smithsons up to dinner as I told you?" asked Miss Cornelia anxiously.

"Yes," was the dreamy response as he glided through the kitchen and vanished into the hall.

Miss Cornelia crimped the edges of her pies delicately with a relieved air. "I made certain he'd forget it," she said. "You just have to watch him as if he were a mere child. Didn't I catch him yesterday starting off to school in his carpet slippers? And in spite of me he got away today in that ridiculous summer hat. You'd better set that jelly in the outpantry to cool, Hannah; it looks good. We'll give those poor little Smithsons a feast for once in their lives if they never get another."

At this juncture the hall door flew open and Mr. Palmer appeared on the threshold. He seemed considerably agitated and for once his eyes had lost their look of space-searching.

"Miss Millar, I am afraid I did make a mistake this morning – it has just dawned on me. I am almost sure that I called at Mrs. Grant's and invited her and her family instead of the Smithsons. And she said they would come."

Miss Cornelia's face was a study.

"Mr. Palmer," she said, flourishing her crimping fork tragically, "do you mean to say you went and invited Linda Grant here tomorrow? Linda Grant, of all women in this world!"

"I did," said the teacher with penitent wretchedness. "It was very careless of me – I am very sorry. What can I do? I'll go down and tell them I made a mistake if you like."

"You can't do that," groaned Miss Cornelia, sitting down and wrinkling up her forehead in dire perplexity. "It would never do in the world. For pity's sake, let me think for a minute."

Miss Cornelia did think – to good purpose evidently, for her forehead smoothed out as her meditations proceeded and her face brightened. Then she got up briskly. "Well, you've done it and no mistake. I don't know that I'm sorry, either. Anyhow, we'll leave it as it is. But you must go straight down now and invite the Smithsons too. And for pity's sake, don't make any more mistakes."

When he had gone Miss Cornelia opened her heart to Hannah. "I never could have done it myself – never; the Turner is too strong in me. But I'm glad it is done. I've been wanting for years to make up with Linda. And now the chance has come, thanks to that blessed blundering boy, I mean to make the most of it. Mind, Hannah, you never whisper a word about its being a mistake. Linda must never know. Poor Linda! She's had a hard time. Hannah, we must make some more pies, and I must go straight down to the store and get some more Santa Claus stuff; I've only got enough to go around the Smithsons."

When Mrs. Grant and her family arrived at the yellow house next morning Miss Cornelia herself ran out bareheaded to meet them. The two women shook hands a little stiffly and then a rill of long-repressed affection trickled out from some secret spring in Miss Cornelia's heart and she kissed her new-found old friend tenderly. Linda returned the kiss warmly, and both felt that the old-time friend-ship was theirs again.

The little Smithsons all came and they and the little Grants sat down on the long bright dining room to a dinner that made history in their small lives, and was eaten over again in happy dreams for months.

How those children did eat! And how beaming Miss Cornelia and grim-faced, soft-hearted Hannah and even the absent-minded teacher himself en-joyed watching them!

After dinner Miss Cornelia distributed among the delighted little souls the presents she had bought for them, and then turned them loose in the big shining kitchen to have a taffy pull – and they had it to their hearts' content! And as for the shocking, taffyfied state into which they got their own rosy faces and that once immaculate domain – well, as Miss Cornelia and Hannah never said one word about it, neither will I.

The four women enjoyed the afternoon in their own way, and the schoolteacher buried himself in algebra to his own great satisfaction.

When her guests went home in the starlit

December dusk, Miss Cornelia walked part of the way with them and had a long confidential talk with Mrs. Grant. When she returned it was to find Hannah groaning in and over the kitchen and the schoolteacher dreamily trying to clean some molasses off his boots with the kitchen hairbrush. Long-suffering Miss Cornelia rescued her property and despatched Mr. Palmer into the woodshed to find the shoe-brush. Then she sat down and laughed.

"Hannah, what will become of that boy yet? There's no counting on what he'll do next. I don't know how he'll ever get through the world, I'm sure, but I'll look after him while he's here at least. I owe him a huge debt of gratitude for this Christmas blunder. What an awful mess this place is in! But, Hannah, did you ever in the world see anything so delightful as that little Tommy Smithson stuffing himself with plum cake, not to mention Teddy Grant? It did me good just to see them."

THE CHRISTMAS SURPRISE
AT ENDERLY ROAD

hil, I'm getting fearfully hungry. When are we going to strike civilization?"

The speaker was my chum, Frank Ward. We were home from our academy for the Christmas holidays and had been amusing ourselves on this sunshiny December afternoon by a tramp through the "back lands," as the barrens that swept away south behind the village were called. They were grown over with scrub maple and spruce, and were quite pathless save for meandering sheep tracks that crossed and recrossed, but led apparently nowhere.

Frank and I did not know exactly where we were, but the back lands were not so extensive but that we would come out somewhere if we kept on. It was getting late and we wished to go home.

"I have an idea that we ought to strike civilization somewhere up the Enderly Road pretty soon," I answered.

"Do you call *that* civilization?" said Frank, with a laugh.

No Blackburn Hill boy was ever known to miss an opportunity of flinging a slur at Enderly Road, even if no Enderly Roader were by to feel the sting.

Enderly Road was a miserable little settlement straggling back from Blackburn Hill. It was a forsaken looking place, and the people, as a rule, were poor and shiftless. Between Blackburn Hill and Enderly Road very little social intercourse existed and, as the Road people resented what they called the pride of Blackburn Hill, there was a good deal of bad feeling between the two districts.

Presently Frank and I came out on the Enderly Road. We sat on the fence a few minutes to rest and discuss our route home. "If we go by the road it's three miles," said Frank. "Isn't there a short cut?"

"There ought to be one by the wood-lane that comes out by Jacob Hart's," I answered, "but I don't know where to strike it."

"Here is someone coming now; we'll inquire," said Frank, looking up the curve of the hard-frozen road. The "someone" was a little girl of about ten years old, who was trotting along with a basketful of school books on her arm. She was a pale, pinched little thing, and her jacket and red hood seemed very old and thin.

"Hello, missy," I said, as she came up, and then I stopped, for I saw she had been crying.

"What is the matter?" asked Frank, who was much more at ease with children than I was, and had always a warm spot in his heart for their small troubles. "Has your teacher kept you in for being naughty?"

The mite dashed her little red knuckles across her eyes and answered indignantly, "No, indeed. I stayed after school with Minnie Lawler to sweep the floor."

"And did you and Minnie quarrel, and is that why you are crying?" asked Frank solemnly.

"Minnie and I *never* quarrel. I am crying because we can't have the school decorated on Monday for the examination, after all. The Dickeys have gone back on us . . . after promising, too," and the tears began to swell up in the blue eyes again.

"Very bad behaviour on the part of the Dickeys," commented Frank. "But can't you decorate the school without them?"

"Why, of course not. They are the only big boys in the school. They said they would cut the boughs, and bring a ladder tomorrow and help us nail the wreaths up, and now they won't . . . and everything is spoiled . . . and Miss Davis will be so disappointed."

By dint of questioning Frank soon found out the whole story. The semi-annual public examination was to be held on Monday afternoon, the day before Christmas. Miss Davis had been drilling her little flock for the occasion; and a program of recitations, speeches, and dialogues had been prepared. Our small informant, whose name was Maggie Bates, together with Minnie Lawler and several other little girls, had conceived the idea that it would be a fine thing to decorate the schoolroom with greens. For this it was necessary to ask the help of the boys. Boys were scarce at Enderly school, but the Dickeys, three in number, had promised to see that the thing was done.

"And now they won't," sobbed Maggie. "Matt Dickey is mad at Miss Davis 'cause she stood him on the floor today for not learning his lesson, and he says he won't do a thing nor let any of the other boys help us. Matt just makes all the boys do as he says. I feel dreadful bad, and so does Minnie."

"Well, I wouldn't cry any more about it," said Frank consolingly. "Crying won't do any good, you know. Can you tell us where to find the wood-lane that cuts across to Blackburn Hill?" Maggie could, and gave us minute directions. So, having thanked her, we left her to pursue her disconsolate way and betook ourselves homeward.

"I would like to spoil Matt Dickey's little game," said Frank. "He is evidently trying to run things at Enderly Road school and revenge himself on the teacher. Let us put a spoke in his wheel and do Maggie a good turn as well."

"Agreed. But how?"

Frank had a plan ready to hand and, when we reached home, we took his sisters, Carrie and Mabel, into our confidence; and the four of us worked to such good purpose all the next day, which was Saturday, that by night everything was in readiness.

At dusk Frank and I set out for the Enderly Road, carrying a basket, a small step-ladder, an unlit lantern, a hammer, and a box of tacks. It was dark when we reached the Enderly Road schoolhouse. Fortunately, it was quite out of sight of any inhabited spot, being surrounded by woods. Hence, mysterious lights in it at strange hours would not be likely to attract attention.

The door was locked, but we easily got in by a window, lighted our lantern, and went to work. The schoolroom was small, and the old-fashioned furniture bore marks of hard usage; but everything was very snug, and the carefully swept floor and dusted desks bore testimony to the neatness of our small friend Maggie and her chum Minnie.

Our basket was full of mottoes made from letters cut out of cardboard and covered with lissome sprays of fir. They were, moreover, adorned with gorgeous pink and red tissue roses, which Carrie and Mabel had contributed. We had considerable trouble in getting them tacked up properly, but when we had succeeded, and had furthermore surmounted doors, windows, and blackboard with wreaths of green, the little Enderly Road schoolroom was quite transformed.

"It looks nice," said Frank in a tone of satisfaction. "Hope Maggie will like it."

We swept up the litter we had made, and then scrambled out of the window.

"I'd like to see Matt Dickey's face when he comes Monday morning," I laughed, as we struck into the back lands.

"I'd like to see that midget of a Maggie's," said Frank. "See here, Phil, let's attend the examination Monday afternoon. I'd like to see our decorations in daylight."

We decided to do so, and also thought of something else. Snow fell all day Sunday, so that, on Monday morning, sleighs had to be brought out. Frank and I drove down to the store and invested a considerable share of our spare cash in a varied assortment of knick-knacks. After dinner we drove through to the Enderly Road schoolhouse, tied our horse in a quiet spot, and went in. Our arrival created quite a sensation for, as a rule, Blackburn Hillites did not patronize Enderly Road functions. Miss Davis, the pale, tired-looking little teacher, was evidently pleased, and we were given seats of honour next to the minister on the platform.

Our decorations really looked very well, and were further enhanced by two large red geraniums in full bloom which, it appeared, Maggie had brought from home to adorn the teacher's desk. The side benches were lined with Enderly Road parents, and all the pupils were in their best attire. Our friend Maggie was there, of course, and she smiled and nodded towards the wreaths when she caught our eyes.

The examination was a decided success, and the program which followed was very creditable indeed. Maggie and Minnie, in particular, covered themselves with glory, both in class and on the platform. At its close, while the minister was making his speech, Frank slipped out; when the minister sat down the door opened and Santa Claus himself, with big fur coat, ruddy mask, and long white beard, strode into the room with a huge basket on his arm, amid a chorus of surprised "Ohs" from old and young.

Wonderful things came out of that basket. There was some little present for every child there – tops,

knives, and whistles for the boys, dolls and ribbons
for the girls, and a "prize" box of candy for everybody, all of which Santa Claus presented with
appropriate remarks. It was an exciting time, and
it would have been hard to decide which were the
most pleased, parents, pupils, or teacher.

In the confusion Santa Claus discreetly disap-
peared, and school was dismissed. Frank, having
tucked his toggery away in the sleigh, was waiting
for us outside, and we were promptly pounced
upon by Maggie and Minnie, whose long braids
were already adorned with the pink silk ribbons
which had been their gifts.

"*You* decorated the school," cried Maggie excit-
edly. "I know you did. I told Minnie it was you the
minute I saw it."

"You're dreaming, child," said Frank.

"Oh, no, I'm not," retorted Maggie shrewdly,
"and wasn't Matt Dickey mad this morning! Oh,
it was such fun. I think you are two real nice boys
and so does Minnie – don't you Minnie?"

Minnie nodded gravely. Evidently Maggie did
the talking in their partnership.

"This has been a splendid examination," said
Maggie, drawing a long breath. "Real Christmassy,
you know. We never had such a good time before."

"Well, it has paid, don't you think?" asked Frank,
as we drove home.

"Rather," I answered.

It did "pay" in other ways than the mere pleasure of it. There was always a better feeling between the Roaders and the Hillites thereafter. The big brothers of the little girls, to whom our Christmas surprise had been such a treat, thought it worth-while to bury the hatchet, and quarrels between the two villages became things of the past.

THE FALSOMS'
CHRISTMAS DINNER

ell, so it's all settled," said Stephen Falsom.

"Yes," assented Alexina. "Yes, it is," she repeated, as if somebody had questioned it. Then Alexina sighed. Whatever "it" was, the fact of its being settled did not seem to bring Alexina any great peace of mind – nor Stephen either, judging from his face, which wore a sort of "suffer and be strong" expression just then. "When do you go?" said Alexina, after a pause, during which she had frowned out of the window and across the Tracy yard. Josephine Tracy and her brother Duncan were strolling about the yard in the pleasant December sunshine, arm in arm, laughing and talking. They appeared to be a nice, harmless pair of people, but the sight of them did not seem to please Alexina.

"Just as soon as we can sell the furniture and

move away," said Stephen moodily. "Heigh-ho! So this is what all our fine ambitions have come to, Lexy, your music and my M.D. A place in a department store for you, and one in a lumber mill for me."

"I don't dare to complain," said Alexina slowly. "We ought to be so thankful to get the positions. I *am* thankful. And I don't mind so very much about my music. But I do wish you could have gone to college, Stephen."

"Never mind me," said Stephen, brightening up determinedly. "I'm going to go into the lumber business enthusiastically. You don't know what unsuspected talents I may develop along that line. The worst of it is that we can't be together. But I'll keep my eyes open, and perhaps I'll find a place for you in Lessing."

Alexina said nothing. Her separation from Stephen was the one point in their fortunes she could not bear to discuss. There were times when Alexina did not see how she was going to exist without Stephen. But she never said so to him. She thought he had enough to worry him without her making matters worse. "Well," said Stephen, getting up, "I'll run down to the office. And see here, Lexy. Day after tomorrow is Christmas. Are we going to celebrate it at all? If so I'd better order the turkey."

Alexina looked thoughtful. "I don't know,

Stephen. We're short of money, you know, and the fund is dwindling every day. Don't you think it's a little extravagant to have a turkey for two people? And somehow I don't feel a bit Christmassy. I think I'd rather spend it just like any other day and try to forget that it *is* Christmas. Everything would be so different."

"That's true, Lexy. And we must look after the bawbees closely, I'll admit." When Stephen had gone out Alexina cried a little, not very much, because she didn't want her eyes to be red against Stephen's return. But she had to cry a little. As she had said, everything was so different from what it had been a year ago. Their father had been alive then and they had been very cosy and happy in the little house at the end of the street. There had been no mother there since Alexina's birth sixteen years ago. Alexina had kept house for her father and Stephen since she was ten. Stephen was a clever boy and intended to study medicine. Alexina had a good voice, and something was to be done about training it. The Tracys lived next door to them. Duncan Tracy was Stephen's particular chum, and Josephine Tracy was Alexina's dearest friend. Alexina was never lonely when Josie was near by to laugh and chat and plan with.

Then, all at once, troubles came. In June the firm of which Mr. Falsom was a member failed. There was some stigma attached to the failure, too, although the blame did not rest upon Mr. Falsom, but with his partner. Worry and anxiety aggravated the heart trouble from which he had suffered for some time, and a month later he died. Alexina and Stephen were left alone to face the knowledge that they were penniless, and must look about for some way of supporting themselves. At first they hoped to be able to get something to do in Thorndale, so that they might keep their home. This proved impossible. After much discouragement and disappointment Stephen had secured a position in the lumber mill at Lessing, and Alexina was promised a place in a departmental store in the city.

To make matters worse, Duncan Tracy and Stephen had quarrelled in October. It was only a boyish disagreement over some trifle, but bitter words had passed. Duncan, who was a quick-tempered lad, had twitted Stephen with his father's failure, and Stephen had resented it hotly. Duncan was sorry for and ashamed of his words as soon as they were uttered, but he would not humble himself to say so. Alexina had taken Stephen's part and her manner to Josie assumed a tinge of coldness. Josie quickly noticed and resented it, and the breach between the two girls widened almost insensibly, until they barely spoke when they met.

Each blamed the other and cherished bitterness in her heart.

When Stephen came home from the post office he looked excited.

"Were there any letters?" asked Alexina.

"Well, rather! One from Uncle James!"

"Uncle James," exclaimed Alexina, incredulously.

"Yes, beloved sis. Oh, you needn't try to look as surprised as I did. And I ordered the turkey after all. Uncle James has invited himself here to dinner on Christmas Day. You'll have a chance to show your culinary skill, for you know we've always been told that Uncle James was a gourmand."

Alexina read the letter in a maze. It was a brief epistle, stating that the writer wished to make the acquaintance of his niece and nephew, and would visit them on Christmas Day. That was all. But Alexina instantly saw a future of rosy possibilities. For Uncle James, who lived in the city and was really a great-uncle, had never taken the slightest notice of their family since his quarrel with their father twenty years ago; but this looked as if Uncle James were disposed to hold out the olive branch.

"Oh, Stephen, if he likes you, and if he offers to educate you!" breathed Alexina. "Perhaps he will if he is favourably impressed. But we'll have to be so careful, he is so whimsical and odd, at least everybody has always said so. A little thing may turn the scale either way. Anyway, we must have a good dinner for him. I'll have plum pudding and mince pie."

For the next thirty-six hours Alexina lived in a whirl. There was so much to do. The little house was put in apple pie order from top to bottom, and Stephen was set to stoning raisins and chopping meat and beating eggs. Alexina was perfectly reckless; no matter how big a hole it made in their finances Uncle James must have a proper Christmas dinner. A favourable impression must be made. Stephen's whole future – Alexina did not think about her own at all just then – might depend on it.

Christmas morning came, fine and bright and warm. It was more like a morning in early spring than in December, for there was no snow or frost, and the air was moist and balmy. Alexina was up at daybreak, cleaning and decorating at a furious rate. By eleven o'clock everything was finished or going forward briskly. The plum pudding was bubbling in the pot, the turkey – Burton's plumpest – was sizzling in the oven. The shelf in the pantry bore two mince pies upon which Alexina was willing to stake her culinary reputation. And Stephen had gone to the train to meet Uncle James.

From her kitchen window Alexina could see brisk preparations going on in the Tracy kitchen. She knew Josie and Duncan were all alone; their parents had gone to spend Christmas with friends in Lessing. In spite of her hurry and excitement Alexina found time to sigh. Last Christmas Josie and Duncan had come over and eaten their dinner with them. But now last Christmas seemed very far away. And Josie had behaved horridly. Alexina was quite clear on that point.

Then Stephen came with Uncle James. Uncle James was a rather pompous, fussy old man with red cheeks and bushy eyebrows. "H'm! Smells nice in here," was his salutation to Alexina. "I hope it will taste as good as it smells. I'm hungry."

Alexina soon left Uncle James and Stephen talking in the parlour and betook herself anxiously to the kitchen. She set the table in the little dining room, now and then pausing to listen with a delighted nod to the murmur of voices and laughter in the parlour. She felt sure that Stephen was making a favourable impression. She lifted the plum pudding and put it on a plate on the kitchen table; then she took out the turkey, beautifully done, and put it on a platter; finally, she popped the two mince pies into the oven. Just at this moment Stephen stuck his head in at the hall door.

"Lexy, do you know where that letter of

Governor Howland's to Father is? Uncle James
wants to see it."

Alexina, not waiting to shut the oven door – for
delay might impress Uncle James unfavourably –
rushed upstairs to get the letter. She was ten minutes finding it. Then, remembering her pies, she
flew back to the kitchen. In the middle of the floor
she stopped as if transfixed, staring at the table. The
turkey was gone. And the plum pudding was gone!
And the mince pies were gone! Nothing was left
but the platters! For a moment Alexina refused to
believe her eyes. Then she saw a trail of greasy
drops on the floor to the open door, out over the
doorstep, and along the boards of the walk to the
back fence.

Alexina did not make a fuss. Even at that horrible moment she remembered the importance of
making a favourable impression. But she could not
quite keep the alarm and excitement out of her
voice as she called Stephen, and Stephen knew that
something had gone wrong as he came quickly
through the hall. "Is the turkey burned, Lexy?" he
cried.

"Burned! No, it's ten times worse," gasped
Alexina. "It's gone – gone, Stephen. And the
pudding and the mince pies, too. Oh, what shall we
do? Who can have taken them?"

It may be stated right here and now that the

Falsoms never really *knew* anything more about the disappearance of their Christmas dinner than they did at that moment. But the only reasonable explanation of the mystery was that a tramp had entered the kitchen and made off with the good things. The Falsom house was right at the end of the street. The narrow backyard opened on a lonely road. Across the road was a stretch of pine woods. There was no house very near except the Tracy one.

Stephen reached this conclusion with a bound. He ran out to the yard gate followed by the distracted Alexina. The only person visible was a man some distance down the road. Stephen leaped over the gate and tore down the road in pursuit of him. Alexina went back to the doorstep, sat down upon it, and began to cry. She couldn't help it. Her hopes were all in ruins around her. There was no dinner for Uncle James.

Josephine Tracy saw her crying. Now, Josie honestly thought that she had a grievance against Alexina. But an Alexina walking unconcernedly by with a cool little nod and her head held high was a very different person from an Alexina sitting on a back doorstep, on Christmas morning, crying. For a moment Josie hesitated. Then she slowly went out and across the yard to the fence. "What is the trouble?" she asked.

Alexina forgot that there was such a thing as dignity to be kept up; or, if she remembered it, she was past caring for such a trifle. "Our dinner is gone," she sobbed. "And there is nothing to give Uncle James to eat except vegetables – and I do so want to make a favourable impression!"

This was not particularly lucid, but Josie, with a flying mental leap, arrived at the conclusion that it was very important that Uncle James, whoever he was, should have a dinner, and she knew where one was to be had. But before she could speak Stephen returned, looking rueful. "No use, Lexy. That man was only old Mr. Byers, and he had seen no signs of a tramp. There is a trail of grease right across the road. The tramp must have taken directly to the woods. We'll simply have to do without our Christmas dinner."

"By no means," said Josie quickly, with a little red spot on either cheek. "Our dinner is all ready – turkey, pudding and all. Let us lend it to you. Don't say a word to your uncle about the accident."

Alexina flushed and hesitated. "It's very kind of you," she stammered, "but I'm afraid – it would be too much –"

"Not a bit of it," Josie interrupted warmly. "Didn't Duncan and I have Christmas dinner at your house last year? Just come and help us carry it over."

"If you lend us your dinner you and Duncan must come and help us eat it," said Alexina, resolutely.

"I'll come of course," said Josie, "and I think that Duncan will too if – if –" She looked at Stephen, the scarlet spots deepening. Stephen coloured too.

"Duncan must come," he said quietly. "I'll go and ask him."

Two minutes later a peculiar procession marched out of the Tracy kitchen door, across the two yards, and into the Falsom house. Josie headed it, carrying a turkey on a platter. Alexina came next with a plum pudding. Stephen and Duncan followed with a hot mince pie apiece. And in a few more minutes Alexina gravely announced to Uncle James that dinner was ready.

The dinner was a pronounced success, marked by much suppressed hilarity among the younger members of the party. Uncle James ate very heartily and seemed to enjoy everything, especially the mince pie.

"This is the best mince pie I have ever sampled," he told Alexina. "I am glad to know that I have a niece who can make such a mince pie." Alexina cast an agonized look at Josie, and was on the point of explaining that she wasn't the maker of the pie. But Josie frowned her into silence.

"I felt so guilty to sit there and take the credit –

your credit," she told Josie afterwards, as they washed up the dishes.

"Nonsense," said Josie. "It wasn't as if you couldn't make mince pies. Your mince pies are better than mine, if it comes to that. It might have spoiled everything if you'd said a word. I must go home now. Won't you and Stephen come over after your uncle goes, and spend the evening with us? We'll have a candy pull."

When Josie and Duncan had gone, Uncle James called his nephew and niece into the parlour, and sat down before them with approving eyes. "I want to have a little talk with you two. I'm sorry I've let so many years go by without making your acquaintance, because you seem worth getting acquainted with. Now, what are your plans for the future?"

"I'm going into a lumber mill at Lessing and Alexina is going into the T. Morson store," said Stephen quietly.

"Tut, tut, no, you're not. And she's not. You're coming to live with me, both of you. If you have a fancy for cutting and carving people up, young man, you must be trained to cut and carve them scientifically, anyhow. As for you, Alexina, Stephen tells me you can sing. Well, there's a good Conservatory of Music in town. Wouldn't you rather go there instead of behind a counter?"

"Oh, Uncle James!" exclaimed Alexina with

shining eyes. She jumped up, put her arms about Uncle James' neck and kissed him.

Uncle James said, "Tut, tut," again, but he liked it.

When Stephen had seen his uncle off on the six o'clock train he returned home and looked at the radiant Alexina.

"Well, you made your favourable impression, all right, didn't you?" he said gaily. "But we owe it to Josie Tracy. Isn't she a brick? I suppose you're going over this evening?"

"Yes, I am. I'm so tired that I feel as if I couldn't crawl across the yard, but if I can't you'll have to carry me. Go I will. I can't begin to tell you how glad I am about everything, but really the fact that you and Duncan and Josie and I are good friends again seems the best of all. I'm glad that tramp stole the dinner and I hope he enjoyed it. I don't grudge him one single bite!"

A CHRISTMAS INSPIRATION

ell, I really think Santa Claus has been very good to us all," said Jean Lawrence, pulling the pins out of her heavy coil of fair hair and letting it ripple over her shoulders.

"So do I," said Nellie Preston as well as she could with a mouthful of chocolates. "Those blessed home folks of mine seem to have divined by instinct the very things I most wanted."

It was the dusk of Christmas Eve and they were all in Jean Lawrence's room at No. 16 Chestnut Terrace. No. 16 was a boarding-house, and boarding-houses are not proverbially cheerful places in which to spend Christmas, but Jean's room, at least, was a pleasant spot, and all the girls had brought their Christmas presents in to show each other. Christmas came on Sunday that year and the

Saturday evening mail at Chestnut Terrace had been an exciting one.

Jean had lighted the pink-globed lamp on her table and the mellow light fell over merry faces as the girls chatted about their gifts. On the table was a big white box heaped with roses that betokened a bit of Christmas extravagance on somebody's part. Jean's brother had sent them to her from Montreal, and all the girls were enjoying them in common.

No. 16 Chestnut Terrace was overrun with girls generally. But just now only five were left; all the others had gone home for Christmas, but these five could not go and were bent on making the best of it.

Belle and Olive Reynolds, who were sitting on the bed – Jean could never keep them off it – were High School girls; they were said to be always laughing, and even the fact that they could not go home for Christmas because a young brother had measles did not dampen their spirits.

Beth Hamilton, who was hovering over the roses, and Nellie Preston, who was eating candy, were art students, and their homes were too far away to visit. As for Jean Lawrence, she was an orphan, and had no home of her own. She worked on the staff of one of the big city newspapers and the other girls were a little in awe of her cleverness, but her nature was a "chummy" one and her room was a favourite rendezvous. Everybody liked frank, open-handed and hearted Jean.

"It was so funny to see the postman when he came this evening," said Olive. "He just bulged with parcels. They were sticking out in every direction."

"We all got our share of them," said Jean with a sigh of content.

"Even the cook got six – I counted."

"Miss Allen didn't get a thing – not even a letter," said Beth quickly. Beth had a trick of seeing things that other girls didn't.

"I forgot Miss Allen. No, I don't believe she did," answered Jean thoughtfully as she twisted up her pretty hair. "How dismal it must be to be so forlorn as that on Christmas Eve of all times. Ugh! I'm glad I have friends."

"I saw Miss Allen watching us as we opened our parcels and letters," Beth went on. "I happened to look up once, and such an expression as was on her face, girls! It was pathetic and sad and envious all at once. It really made me feel bad – for five minutes," she concluded honestly.

"Hasn't Miss Allen any friends at all?" asked Beth.

"No, I don't think she has," answered Jean. "She has lived here for fourteen years, so Mrs. Pickrell says. Think of that, girls! Fourteen years at Chestnut Terrace! Is it any wonder that she is thin and dried-up and snappy?"

"Nobody ever comes to see her and she never goes anywhere," said Beth. "Dear me! She must feel lonely now when everybody else is being remembered by their friends. I can't forget her face tonight; it actually haunts me. Girls, how would you feel if you hadn't anyone belonging to you, and if nobody thought about you at Christmas?"

"Ow!" said Olive, as if the mere idea made her shiver.

A little silence followed. To tell the truth, none of them liked Miss Allen. They knew that she did not like them either, but considered them frivolous and pert, and complained when they made a racket.

"The skeleton at the feast," Jean called her, and certainly the presence of the pale, silent, discontented-looking woman at the No. 16 table did not tend to heighten its festivity.

Presently Jean said with a dramatic flourish, "Girls, I have an inspiration – a Christmas inspiration!"

"What is it?" cried four voices.

"Just this. Let us give Miss Allen a Christmas surprise. She has not received a single present and

I'm sure she feels lonely. Just think how we would feel if we were in her place."

"That is true," said Olive thoughtfully. "Do you know, girls, this evening I went to her room with a message from Mrs. Pickrell, and I do believe she had been crying. Her room looked dreadfully bare and cheerless, too. I think she is very poor. What are we to do, Jean?"

"Let us each give her something nice. We can put the things just outside of her door so that she will see them whenever she opens it. I'll give her some of Fred's roses too, and I'll write a Christmassy letter in my very best style to go with them," said Jean, warming up to her ideas as she talked.

The other girls caught her spirit and entered into the plan with enthusiasm.

"Splendid!" cried Beth. "Jean, it is an inspiration, sure enough. Haven't we been horribly selfish – thinking of nothing but our own gifts and fun and pleasure? I really feel ashamed."

"Let us do the thing up the very best way we can," said Nellie, forgetting even her beloved chocolates in her eagerness. "The shops are open yet. Let us go up town and invest."

Five minutes later five capped and jacketed figures were scurrying up the street in the frosty, starlit December dusk. Miss Allen in her cold little room heard their gay voices and sighed. She was crying by herself in the dark. It was Christmas for everybody but her, she thought drearily.

In an hour the girls came back with their purchases.

"Now, let's hold a council of war," said Jean jubilantly. "I hadn't the faintest idea what Miss Allen would like so I just guessed wildly. I got her a lace handkerchief and a big bottle of perfume and a painted photograph frame – and I'll stick my own photo in it for fun. That was really all I could afford. Christmas purchases have left my purse dreadfully lean."

"I got her a glove-box and a pin tray," said Belle, "and Olive got her a calendar and Whittier's poems. And besides we are going to give her half of that big plummy fruit cake Mother sent us from home. I'm sure she hasn't tasted anything so delicious for years, for fruit cakes don't grow on Chestnut Terrace and she never goes anywhere else for a meal."

Beth had bought a pretty cup and saucer and said she meant to give one of her pretty water-colours too. Nellie, true to her reputation, had invested in a big box of chocolate creams, a gorgeously striped candy cane, a bag of oranges, and a brilliant lampshade of rose-coloured crepe paper to top off with.

"It makes such a lot of show for the money," she explained. "I am bankrupt, like Jean."

"Well, we've got a lot of pretty things," said Jean

in a tone of satisfaction. "Now we must do them up nicely. Will you wrap them in tissue paper, girls, and tie them with baby ribbon – here's a box of it – while I write that letter?"

While the others chatted over their parcels Jean wrote her letter, and Jean could write delightful letters. She had a decided talent in that respect, and her correspondents all declared her letters to be things of beauty and joy forever. She put her best into Miss Allen's Christmas letter. Since then she has written many bright and clever things, but I do not believe she ever in her life wrote anything more genuinely original and delightful than that letter. Besides, it breathed the very spirit of Christmas, and all the girls declared that it was splendid.

"You must all sign it now," said Jean, "and I'll put it in one of those big envelopes; and, Nellie, won't you write her name on it in fancy letters?"

Which Nellie proceeded to do, and furthermore embellished the envelope by a border of chubby cherubs, dancing hand in hand around it and a sketch of No. 16 Chestnut Terrace in the corner in lieu of a stamp. Not content with this she hunted out a huge sheet of drawing paper and drew upon it an original pen-and-ink design after her own heart. A dudish cat – Miss Allen was fond of the No. 16 cat if she could be said to be fond of anything – was portrayed seated on a rocker arrayed in smoking jacket and cap with a cigar waved airily aloft in one paw while the other held out a placard bearing the legend "Merry Christmas." A second cat in full street costume bowed politely, hat in paw, and waved a banner inscribed with "Happy New Year," while faintly suggested kittens gambolled around the border. The girls laughed until they cried over it and voted it to be the best thing Nellie had yet done in original work.

All this had taken time and it was past eleven o'clock. Miss Allen had cried herself to sleep long ago and everybody else in Chestnut Terrace was abed when five figures cautiously crept down the hall, headed by Jean with a dim lamp. Outside of Miss Allen's door the procession halted and the girls silently arranged their gifts on the floor.

"That's done," whispered Jean in a tone of satisfaction as they tiptoed back. "And now let us go to bed or Mrs. Pickrell, bless her heart, will be down on us for burning so much midnight oil. Oil has gone up, you know, girls."

It was in the early morning that Miss Allen opened her door. But early as it was, another door down the hall was half open too and five rosy faces were peering cautiously out. The girls had been up for an hour for fear they would miss the sight and were all in Nellie's room, which commanded a view of Miss Allen's door.

That lady's face was a study. Amazement, incredulity, wonder, chased each other over it, succeeded by a glow of pleasure. On the floor before her was a snug little pyramid of parcels topped by Jean's letter. On a chair behind it was a bowl of delicious hot-house roses and Nellie's placard.

Miss Allen looked down the hall but saw nothing, for Jean had slammed the door just in time. Half an hour later when they were going down to breakfast Miss Allen came along the hall with outstretched hands to meet them. She had been crying again, but I think her tears were happy ones; and she was smiling now. A cluster of Jean's roses were pinned on her breast.

"Oh, girls, girls," she said, with a little tremble in her voice, "I can never thank you enough. It was so kind and sweet of you. You don't know how much good you have done me."

Breakfast was an unusually cheerful affair at No. 16 that morning. There was no skeleton at the feast and everybody was beaming. Miss Allen laughed and talked like a girl herself.

"Oh, how surprised I was!" she said. "The roses were like a bit of summer, and those cats of Nellie's were so funny and delightful. And your letter too, Jean! I cried and laughed over it. I shall read it every day for a year."

After breakfast everyone went to Christmas

service. The girls went uptown to the church they attended. The city was very beautiful in the morning sunshine. There had been a white frost in the night and the tree-lined avenues and public squares seemed like glimpses of fairyland.

"How lovely the world is," said Jean.

"This is really the very happiest Christmas morning I have ever known," declared Nellie. "I never felt so really Christmassy in my inmost soul before."

"I suppose," said Beth thoughtfully, "that it is because we have discovered for ourselves the old truth that it is more blessed to give than to receive. I've always known it, in a way, but I never realized it before."

"Blessing on Jean's Christmas inspiration," said Nellie. "But, girls, let us try to make it an all-the-year-round inspiration, I say. We can bring a little of our own sunshine into Miss Allen's life as long as we live with her."

"Amen to that!" said Jean heartily. "Oh, listen, girls – the Christmas chimes!"

And over all the beautiful city was wafted the grand old message of peace on earth and good will to all the world.

THE JOSEPHS' CHRISTMAS

 he month before Christmas was always the most exciting and mysterious time in the Joseph household. Such scheming and planning, such putting of curly heads together in corners, such counting of small hoards, such hiding and smuggling of things out of sight, as went on among the little Josephs!

There were a good many of them, and very few of the pennies; hence the reason for so much contriving and consulting. From fourteen-year-old Mollie down to four-year-old Lennie there were eight small Josephs in all in the little log house on the prairie; so that when each little Joseph wanted to give a Christmas box to each of the other little Josephs, and something to Father and Mother Joseph besides, it is no wonder that they had to cudgel their small brains for ways and means thereof.

Father and Mother were always discreetly blind and silent through December. No questions were asked no matter what queer things were done. Many secret trips to the little store at the railway station two miles away were ignored, and no little Joseph was called to account because he or she looked terribly guilty when somebody suddenly came into the room. The air was simply charged with secrets.

Sister Mollie was the grand repository of these; all the little Josephs came to her for advice and assistance. It was Mollie who for troubled small brothers and sisters did such sums in division as this: How can I get a ten-cent present for Emmy and a fifteen-cent one for Jimmy out of eighteen cents? Or, how can seven sticks of candy be divided among eight people so that each shall have one? It was Mollie who advised regarding the purchase of ribbon and crepe paper. It was Mollie who put the finishing touches to most of the little gifts. In short, all through December Mollie was weighed down under an avalanche of responsibility. It speaks volumes for her sagacity and skill that she never got things mixed up or made any such terrible mistake as letting one little Joseph find out what another was going to give him. "Dead" secrecy was the keystone of all plans and confidences.

During this particular December the planning and contriving had been more difficult and the results less satisfactory than usual. The Josephs were poor at any time, but this winter they were poorer than ever. The crops had failed in the summer, and as a consequence the family were, as Jimmy said, "on short commons." But they made the brave best of their small resources, and on Christmas Eve every little Joseph went to bed with a clear conscience, for was there not on the corner table in the kitchen a small mountain of tiny – sometimes very tiny – gifts labelled with the names of recipients and givers, and worth their weight in gold if love and good wishes count for anything?

It was beginning to snow when the small small Josephs went to bed, and when the big small Josephs climbed the stairs it was snowing thickly. Mr. and Mrs. Joseph sat before the fire and listened to the wind howling about the house.

"I'm glad I'm not driving over the prairie tonight," said Mr. Joseph. "It's quite a storm. I hope it will be fine tomorrow, for the children's sake. They've set their hearts on having a sleigh ride, and it will be too bad if they can't have it when it's about all the Christmas they'll have this year. Mary,

this is the first Christmas since we came west that
we couldn't afford some little extras for them, even
if 'twas only a box of nuts and candy."

Mrs. Joseph sighed over Jimmy's worn jacket
which she was mending. Then she smiled.

"Never mind, John. Things will be better next
Christmas, we'll hope. The children will not mind,
bless their hearts. Look at all the little knick-knacks
they've made for each other. Last week when I was
over at Taunton, Mr. Fisher had his store all 'gayi-
fied up,' as Jim says, with Christmas presents. I did
feel that I'd ask nothing better than to go in and buy
all the lovely things I wanted, just for once, and give
them to the children tomorrow morning. They've
never had anything really nice for Christmas. But
there! We've all got each other and good health and
spirits, and a Christmas wouldn't be much without
those if we had all the presents in the world."

Mr. Joseph nodded.

"That's so. I don't want to grumble; but I tell you
I did want to get Maggie a 'real live doll,' as she calls
it. She never has had anything but homemade dolls,
and that small heart of hers is set on a real one.
There was one at Fisher's store today – a big beauty
with real hair, and eyes that opened and shut. Just
fancy Maggie's face if she saw such a Christmas box
as that tomorrow morning."

"Don't let's fancy it," laughed Mrs. Joseph, "it

is only aggravating. Talking of candy reminds me that I made a big plateful of taffy for the children today. It's all the 'Christmassy' I could give them. I'll get it out and put it on the table along with the children's presents. That can't be someone at the door!"

"It is, though," said Mr. Joseph as he strode to the door and flung it open.

Two snowed-up figures were standing on the porch. As they stepped in, the Josephs recognized one of them as Mr. Ralston, a wealthy merchant in a small town fifteen miles away.

"Late hour for callers, isn't it?" said Mr. Ralston. "The fact is, our horse has about given out, and the storm is so bad that we can't proceed. This is my wife, and we are on our way to spend Christmas with my brother's family at Lindsay. Can you take us in for the night, Mr. Joseph?"

"Certainly, and welcome!" exclaimed Mr. Joseph heartily, "if you don't mind a shakedown by the kitchen fire for the night. My, Mrs. Ralston," as his wife helped her off with her things, "but you are snowed up! I'll see to putting your horse away, Mr. Ralston. This way, if you please."

When the two men came stamping into the house again Mrs. Ralston and Mrs. Joseph were sitting at the fire, the former with a steaming hot cup of tea in her hand. Mr. Ralston put the big basket he was carrying down on a bench in the corner.

"Thought I'd better bring our Christmas flummery in," he said. "You see, Mrs. Joseph, my brother has a big family, so we are taking them a lot of Santa Claus stuff. Mrs. Ralston packed this basket, and goodness knows what she put in it, but she half cleaned out my store. The eyes of the Lindsay youngsters will dance tomorrow – that is, if we ever get there."

Mrs. Joseph gave a little sigh in spite of herself, and looked wistfully at the heap of gifts on the corner table. How meagre and small they did look, to be sure, beside that bulgy basket with its cover suggestively tied down.

Mrs. Ralston looked too.

"Santa Claus seems to have visited you already," she said with a smile.

The Josephs laughed.

"Our Santa Claus is somewhat out of pocket this year," said Mr. Joseph frankly. "Those are the little things the small folks here have made for each other. They've been a month at it, and I'm always kind of relieved when Christmas is over and there are no more mysterious doings. We're in such cramped quarters here that you can't move without stepping on somebody's secret."

A shakedown was spread in the kitchen for the unexpected guests, and presently the Ralstons found themselves alone. Mrs. Ralston went over to the Christmas table and looked at the little gifts half tenderly and half pityingly.

"They're not much like the contents of our basket, are they?" she said, as she touched the calendar Jimmie had made for Mollie out of cardboard and autumn leaves and grasses.

"Just what I was thinking," returned her husband, "and I was thinking of something else, too. I've a notion that I'd like to see some of the things in our basket right here on this table."

"I'd like to see them all," said Mrs. Ralston promptly. "Let's just leave them here, Edward. Roger's family will have plenty of presents without them, and for that matter we can send them ours when we go back home."

"Just as you say," agreed Mr. Ralston. "I like the idea of giving the small folk of this household a rousing good Christmas for once. They're poor I know, and I dare say pretty well pinched this year like most of the farmers hereabout after the crop failure."

Mrs. Ralston untied the cover of the big basket. Then the two of them, moving as stealthily as if engaged in a burglary, transferred the contents to the table. Mr. Ralston got out a small pencil and a note book, and by dint of comparing the names attached to the gifts on the table they managed to divide theirs up pretty evenly among the little Josephs.

When all was done Mrs. Ralston said, "Now, I'm going to spread that tablecloth carelessly over the table. We will be going before daylight, probably, and in the hurry of getting off I hope that Mr. and Mrs. Joseph will not notice the difference till we're gone."

It fell out as Mrs. Ralston had planned. The dawn broke fine and clear over a vast white world. Mr. and Mrs. Joseph were early astir; breakfast for the storm-stayed travellers was cooked and eaten by lamplight; then the horse and sleigh were brought to the door and Mr. Ralston carried out his empty basket.

"I expect the trail will be heavy," he said, "but I guess we'd get to Lindsay in time for dinner, anyway. Much obliged for your kindness, Mr. Joseph. When you and Mrs. Joseph come to town we shall hope to have a chance to return it. Good-bye and a merry Christmas to you all."

When Mrs. Joseph went back to the kitchen her eyes fell on the heaped-up table in the corner.

"Why-y!" she said, and snatched off the cover.

One look she gave, and then this funny little

mother began to cry; but they were happy tears. Mr. Joseph came too, and looked and whistled.

There really seemed to be everything on that table that the hearts of children could desire – three pairs of skates, a fur cap and collar, a dainty work-basket, half a dozen gleaming new books, a writing desk, a roll of stuff that looked like a new dress, a pair of fur-topped kid gloves just Mollie's size, and a china cup and saucer. All these were to be seen at the first glance; and in one corner of the table was a big box filled with candies and nuts and raisins, and in the other a doll with curling golden hair and brown eyes, dressed in "real" clothes and with all her wardrobe in a trunk beside her. Pinned to her dress was a leaf from Mr. Ralston's notebook with Maggie's name written on it.

"Well, this is Christmas with a vengeance," said Mr. Joseph.

"The children will go wild with delight," said his wife happily.

They pretty nearly did when they all came scrambling down the stairs a little later. Such a Christmas had never been known in the Joseph household before. Maggie clasped her doll with shining eyes, Mollie looked at the workbasket that her housewifely little heart had always longed for, studious Jimmy beamed over the books, and Ted and Hal whooped with delight over the skates. And as for the big box of good things, why, everybody appreciated that. That Christmas was one to date from in that family.

I'm glad to be able to say, too, that even in the heyday of their delight and surprise over their wonderful presents, the little Josephs did not forget to appreciate the gifts they had prepared for each other. Mollie thought her calendar just too pretty for anything, and Jimmy was sure the new red mittens which Maggie had knitted for him with her own chubby wee fingers, were the very nicest, gayest mittens a boy had ever worn.

Mrs. Joseph's taffy was eaten too. Not a scrap of it was left. As Ted said loyally, "It was just as good as the candy in the box and had more 'chew' to it besides."

UNCLE RICHARD'S
NEW YEAR'S DINNER

rissy Baker was in Oscar Miller's store New Year's morning, buying matches — for New Year's was not kept as a business holiday in Quincy — when her uncle, Richard Baker, came in. He did not look at Prissy, nor did she wish him a happy New Year; she would not have dared. Uncle Richard had not been on speaking terms with her or her father, his only brother, for eight years.

He was a big, ruddy, prosperous-looking man — an uncle to be proud of, Prissy thought wistfully, if only he were like other people's uncles, or, indeed, like what he used to be himself. He was the only uncle Prissy had, and when she had been a little girl they had been great friends; but that was before the quarrel, in which Prissy had had no share, to be sure, although Uncle Richard seemed to include her in his rancour.

Richard Baker, so he informed Mr. Miller, was on his way to Navarre with a load of pork.

"I didn't intend going over until the afternoon," he said, "but Joe Hemming sent word yesterday he wouldn't be buying pork after twelve today. So I have to tote my hogs over at once. I don't care about doing business New Year's morning."

"Should think New Year's would be pretty much the same as any other day to you," said Mr. Miller, for Richard Baker was a bachelor, with only old Mrs. Janeway to keep house for him.

"Well, I always like a good dinner on New Year's," said Richard Baker. "It's about the only way I can celebrate. Mrs. Janeway wanted to spend the day with her son's family over at Oriental, so I was laying out to cook my own dinner. I got everything ready in the pantry last night, 'fore I got word about the pork. I won't get back from Navarre before one o'clock, so I reckon I'll have to put up with a cold bite."

After her Uncle Richard had driven away, Prissy walked thoughtfully home. She had planned to spend a nice, lazy holiday with the new book her father had given her at Christmas and a box of candy. She did not even mean to cook a dinner, for her father had had to go to town that morning to meet a friend and would be gone the whole day. There was nobody else to cook dinner for. Prissy's mother had died when Prissy was a baby. She was her father's housekeeper, and they had jolly times together.

But as she walked home, she could not help thinking about Uncle Richard. He would certainly have cold New Year cheer, enough to chill the whole coming year. She felt sorry for him, picturing him returning from Navarre, cold and hungry, to find a fireless house and an uncooked dinner in the pantry.

Suddenly an idea popped into Prissy's head. Dared she? Oh, she never could! But he would never know – there would be plenty of time – she would!

Prissy hurried home, put her matches away, took a regretful peep at her unopened book, then locked the door and started up the road to Uncle Richard's house half a mile away. She meant to go and cook Uncle Richard's dinner for him, get it all beautifully ready, then slip away before he came home. He would never suspect her of it. Prissy would not have him suspect for the world; she thought he would be more likely to throw a dinner of her cooking out of doors than to eat it.

Eight years before this, when Prissy had been nine years old, Richard and Irving Baker had quarrelled over the division of a piece of property. The fault had been mainly on Richard's side, and that very fact made him all the more unrelenting and stubborn. He had never spoken to his brother since, and he declared he never would. Prissy and her father felt very badly over it, but Uncle Richard did not seem to feel badly at all. To all appearance he had completely forgotten that there were such people in the world as his brother Irving and his niece Prissy.

Prissy had no trouble in breaking into Uncle Richard's house, for the woodshed door was unfastened. She tripped into the hostile kitchen with rosy cheeks and mischief sparkling in her eyes. This was an adventure – this was fun! She would tell her father all about it when he came home at night and what a laugh they would have!

There was still a good fire in the stove, and in the pantry Prissy found the dinner in its raw state – a fine roast of fresh pork, potatoes, cabbage, turnips and the ingredients of a raisin pudding, for Richard Baker was fond of raisin puddings, and could make them as well as Mrs. Janeway could, if that was anything to boast of.

In a short time the kitchen was full of bubbling and hissings and appetizing odours. Prissy enjoyed herself hugely, and the raisin pudding, which she rather doubtfully mixed up, behaved itself beautifully.

"Uncle Richard said he'd be home by one," said Prissy to herself, as the clock struck twelve, "so I'll set the table now, dish up the dinner, and leave it where it will keep warm until he gets here. Then I'll slip away home. I'd like to see his face when he steps in. I suppose he'll think one of the Jenner girls across the street has cooked his dinner."

Prissy soon had the table set, and she was just peppering the turnips when a gruff voice behind her said:

"Well, well, what does this mean?"

Prissy whirled around as if she had been shot, and there stood Uncle Richard in the woodshed door!

Poor Prissy! She could not have looked or felt more guilty if Uncle Richard had caught her robbing his desk. She did not drop the turnips for a wonder; but she was too confused to set them down, so she stood there holding them, her face crimson, her heart thumping, and a horrible choking in her throat.

"I – I – came up to cook your dinner for you, Uncle Richard," she stammered. "I heard you say – in the store – that Mrs. Janeway had gone home and that you had nobody to cook your New Year's dinner for you. So I thought I'd come and do it, but I meant to slip away before you came home."

Poor Prissy felt that she would never get to the end of her explanation. Would Uncle Richard be angry? Would he order her from the house?

"It was very kind of you," said Uncle Richard drily. "It's a wonder your father let you come."

"Father was not home, but I am sure he would not have prevented me if he had been. Father has no hard feelings against you, Uncle Richard."

"Humph!" said Uncle Richard. "Well, since you've cooked the dinner you must stop and help me eat it. It smells good, I must say. Mrs. Janeway always burns pork when she roasts it. Sit down, Prissy. I'm hungry."

They sat down. Prissy felt quite giddy and breathless, and could hardly eat for excitement; but Uncle Richard had evidently brought home a good appetite from Navarre, and he did full justice to his New Year's dinner. He talked to Prissy too, quite kindly and politely, and when the meal was over he said slowly:

"I'm much obliged to you, Prissy, and I don't mind owning to you that I'm sorry for my share in the quarrel, and have wanted for a long time to be friends with your father again, but I was too ashamed and proud to make the first advance. You can tell him so for me, if you like. And if he's willing to let bygones be bygones, tell him I'd like him to come up here with you tonight when he gets home and spend the evening with me."

"Oh, he will come, I know!" cried Prissy joyfully. "He has felt so badly about not being friendly with you, Uncle Richard. I'm as glad as can be."

Prissy ran impulsively around the table and kissed Uncle Richard. He looked up at his tall, girlish niece with a smile of pleasure.

"You're a good girl, Prissy, and a kind-hearted one too, or you'd never have come up here to cook a dinner for a crabbed old uncle who deserved to eat cold dinners for his stubbornness. It made me cross today when folks wished me a happy New Year. It seemed like mockery when I hadn't a soul belonging to me to make it happy. But it has brought me happiness already, and I believe it will be a happy year all the way through."

"Indeed it will!" laughed Prissy. "I'm so happy now I could sing. I believe it was an inspiration — my idea of coming up here to cook your dinner for you."

"You must promise to come and cook my New Year's dinner for me every New Year we live near enough together," said Uncle Richard.

And Prissy promised.

IDA'S NEW YEAR CAKE

Mary Craig and Sara Reid and Josie Pye had all flocked into Ida Mitchell's room at their boarding-house to condole with each other because none of them was able to go home for New Year's. Mary and Josie had been home for Christmas, so they didn't really feel so badly off. But Ida and Sara hadn't even that consolation.

Ida was a third-year student at the Clifton Academy; she had holidays, and nowhere, so she mournfully affirmed, to spend them. At home three brothers and a sister were down with the measles, and, as Ida had never had them, she could not go there; and the news had come too late for her to make any other arrangements.

Mary and Josie were clerks in a Clifton book-store, and Sara was stenographer in a Clifton

lawyer's office. And they were all jolly and thoughtless and very fond of one another.

"This will be the first New Year's I have ever
spent away from home," sighed Sara, nibbling
chocolate fudge. "It does make me so blue to think
of it. And not even a holiday – I'll have to go to
work just the same. Now Ida here, she doesn't really
need sympathy. She has holidays – a whole fortnight
– and nothing to do but enjoy them."

"Holidays are dismal things when you've
nowhere to holiday," said Ida mournfully. "The
time drags horribly. But never mind, girls, I've a
plummy bit of news for you. I'd a letter from
Mother today and, bless the dear woman, she is
sending me a cake – a New Year's cake – a great big,
spicy, mellow, delicious fruit cake. It will be along
tomorrow and, girls, we'll celebrate when it comes.
I've asked everybody in the house up to my room
for New Year's Eve, and we'll have a royal good
time."

"How splendid!" said Mary. "There's nothing I
like more than a slice of real countrified home-
made fruit cake, where they don't scrimp on eggs
or butter or raisins. You'll give me a good big piece,
won't you, Ida?"

"As much as you can eat," promised Ida. "I
can warrant Mother's fruit cake. Yes, we'll have a

jamboree. Miss Monroe has promised to come in too. She says she has a weakness for fruit cake."

"Oh!" breathed all the girls. Miss Monroe was their idol, whom they had to be content to worship at a distance as a general thing. She was a clever journalist, who worked on a paper, and was reputed to be writing a book. The girls felt they were highly privileged to be boarding in the same house, and counted that day lost on which they did not receive a businesslike nod or an absent-minded smile from Miss Monroe. If she ever had time to speak to one of them about the weather, that fortunate one put on airs for a week. And now to think that she had actually promised to drop into Ida's room on New Year's Eve and eat fruit cake!

"There goes that funny little namesake of yours, Ida," said Josie, who was sitting by the window. "She seems to be staying in town over the holidays too. Wonder why. Perhaps she doesn't belong any-where. She really is a most forlorn-appearing little mortal."

There were two Ida Mitchells attending the Clifton Academy. The other Ida was a plain, quiet, pale-faced little girl of fifteen who was in the second year. Beyond that, none of the third-year Ida Mitchell's set knew anything about her, or tried to find out.

"She must be very poor," said Ida carelessly. "She dresses so shabbily, and she always looks so pinched and subdued. She boards in a little house out on Marlboro Road, and I pity her if she has to spend her holidays there, for a more dismal place I never saw. I was there once on the trail of a book I had lost. Going, girls? Well, don't forget tomorrow night."

Ida spent the next day decorating her room and watching for the arrival of her cake. It hadn't come by tea-time, and she concluded to go down to the express office and investigate. It would be dreadful if that cake didn't turn up in time, with all the girls and Miss Monroe coming in. Ida felt that she would be mortified to death.

Inquiry at the express office discovered two things. A box had come in for Miss Ida Mitchell, Clifton; and said box had been delivered to Miss Ida Mitchell, Clifton.

"One of our clerks said he knew you person-ally – boarded next door to you – and he'd take it round himself," the manager informed her.

"There must be some mistake," said Ida in per-plexity. "I don't know any of the clerks here. Oh – why – there's another Ida Mitchell in town! Can it be possible my cake has gone to her?"

The manager thought it very possible, and

offered to send around and see. But Ida said it was on her way home and she would call herself.

At the dismal little house on Marlboro Road she was sent up three flights of stairs to the other Ida Mitchell's small hall bedroom. The other Ida Mitchell opened the door for her. Behind her, on the table, was the cake – such a fine, big, brown cake, with raisins sticking out all over it!

"Why, how do you do, Miss Mitchell!" exclaimed the other Ida with shy pleasure. "Come in. I didn't know you were in town. It's real good of you to come and see me. And just see what I've had sent to me! Isn't it a beauty? I was so surprised when it came – and, oh, so glad! I was feeling so blue and lonesome – as if I hadn't a friend in the world. I – I – yes, I was crying when that cake came. It has just made the world over for me. Do sit down and I'll cut you a piece. I'm sure you're as fond of fruit cake as I am."

Ida sat down in a chair, feeling bewildered and awkward. This was a nice predicament! How could she tell that other Ida that the cake didn't belong to her? The poor thing was so delighted. And, oh, what a bare, lonely little room! The big, luxurious cake seemed to emphasize the bareness and loneliness.

"Who – who sent it to you?" she asked lamely.

"It must have been Mrs. Henderson, because there is nobody else who would," answered the other Ida. "Two years ago I was going to school in Trenton and I boarded with her. When I left her to come to Clifton she told me she would send me a cake for Christmas. Well, I expected that cake last year – and it didn't come. I can't tell you how disappointed I was. You'll think me very childish. But I was so lonely, with no home to go to like the other girls. But she sent it this year, you see. It is so nice to think that somebody has remembered me at New Year's. It isn't the cake itself – it's the thought behind it. It has just made all the difference in the world. There – just sample it, Miss Mitchell."

The other Ida cut a generous slice from the cake and passed it to her guest. Her eyes were shining and her cheeks were flushed. She was really a very sweet-looking little thing – not a bit like her usual pale, timid self.

Ida ate the cake slowly. What was she to do? She couldn't tell the other Ida the truth about the cake. But the girls she had asked in to help eat it that very evening! And Miss Monroe! Oh, dear, it was too bad. But it couldn't be helped. She wouldn't blot out that light on the other Ida's face for anything! Of course, she would find out the truth in time – probably after she had written to thank Mrs. Henderson for the cake; but meanwhile she would have enjoyed the cake, and the supposed kindness back of it would tide her over her New Year loneliness.

"It's delicious," said Ida heartily, swallowing her own disappointment with the cake. "I'm – I'm glad I happened to drop in as I was passing." Ida hoped that speech didn't come under the head of a fib.

"So am I," said the other Ida brightly. "Oh, I've been so lonesome and downhearted this week. I'm so alone, you see – there isn't anybody to care. Father died three years ago, and I don't remember my mother at all. There is nobody but myself, and it is dreadfully lonely at times. When the Academy is open and I have my lessons to study, I don't mind so much. But the holidays take all the courage out of me."

"We should have fraternized more this week," smiled Ida, regretting that she hadn't thought of it before. "I couldn't go home because of the measles, and I've moped a lot. We might have spent the time together and had a real nice, jolly holiday."

The other Ida blushed with delight.

"I'd love to be friends with you," she said slowly. "I've often thought I'd like to know you. Isn't it odd that we have the same name? It was so nice of you to come and see me. I – I'd love to have you come often."

"I will," said Ida heartily.

"Perhaps you will stay the evening," suggested the other Ida. "I've asked some of the girls who board here in to have some cake, I'm so glad to be able to give them something – they've all been so good to me. They are all clerks in stores and some of them are so tired and lonely. It's so nice to have a pleasure to share with them. Won't you stay?"

"I'd like to," laughed Ida, "but I have some guests of my own invited in for tonight. I must hurry home, for they will most surely be waiting for me."

She laughed again as she thought what else the guests would be waiting for. But her face was sober enough as she walked home.

"But I'm glad I left the cake with her," she said resolutely. "Poor little thing! It means so much to her. It meant only 'a good feed,' as Josie says, to me. I'm simply going to make it my business next term to be good friends with the other Ida Mitchell. I'm afraid we third-year girls are very self-centred and selfish. And I know what I'll do! I'll write to Abby Morton in Trenton to send me Mrs. Henderson's address, and I'll write her a letter and ask her not to let Ida know she didn't send the cake."

Ida went into a confectionery store and invested in what Josie Pye was wont to call "ready-to-wear eatables" – fancy cakes, fruit, and candies. When she reached her room she found it full of expectant girls, with Miss Monroe enthroned in the midst of them – Miss Monroe in a wonderful evening dress of black lace and yellow silk, with roses in her hair and pearls on her neck – all donned in honour of Ida's little celebration. I won't say that, just for a moment, Ida didn't regret that she had given up her cake.

"Good evening, Miss Mitchell," cried Mary Craig gaily. "Walk right in and make yourself at home in your own room, do! We all met in the hall, and knocked and knocked. Finally Miss Monroe came, so we made bold to walk right in. Where is the only and original fruit cake, Ida? My mouth has been watering all day."

"The other Ida Mitchell is probably entertaining her friends at this moment with my fruit cake," said Ida, with a little laugh.

Then she told the whole story.

"I'm so sorry to disappoint you," she concluded, "but I simply couldn't tell that poor, lonely child that the cake wasn't intended for her. I've brought all the goodies home with me that I could buy, and we'll have to do the best we can without the fruit cake."

Their "best" proved to be a very good thing. They had a jolly New Year's Eve, and Miss Monroe sparkled and entertained most brilliantly. They kept their celebration up until twelve to welcome the new year in, and then they bade Ida good night.

But Miss Monroe lingered for a moment behind the others to say softly:

"I want to tell you how good and sweet I think it was of you to give up your cake to the other Ida. That little bit of unselfishness was a good guerdon for your new year."

And Ida, radiant-faced at this praise from her idol, answered heartily:

"I'm afraid I'm anything but unselfish, Miss Monroe. But I mean to try to be more this coming year and think a little about the girls outside of my own little set who may be lonely or discouraged. The other Ida Mitchell isn't going to have to depend on that fruit cake alone for comfort and encouragement for the next twelve months."

BERTIE'S NEW YEAR

He stood on the sagging doorstep and looked out on the snowy world. His hands were clasped behind him, and his thin face wore a thoughtful, puzzled look. The door behind him opened jerkingly, and a scowling woman came out with a pan of dishwater in her hand.

"Ain't you gone yet, Bert?" she said sharply. "What in the world are you hanging round for?"

"It's early yet," said Bertie cheerfully. "I thought maybe George Fraser'd be along and I'd get a lift as far as the store."

"Well, I never saw such laziness! No wonder old Sampson won't keep you longer than the holidays if you're no smarter than that. Goodness, if I don't settle that boy!" – as the sound of fretful crying came from the kitchen behind her.

"What is wrong with William John?" asked Bertie.

"Why, he wants to go out coasting with those Robinson boys, but he can't. He hasn't got any mittens and he would catch his death of cold again."

Her voice seemed to imply that William John had died of cold several times already.

Bertie looked soberly down at his old, well-darned mittens. It was very cold, and he would have a great many errands to run. He shivered, and looked up at his aunt's hard face as she stood wiping her dish-pan with a grim frown which boded no good to the discontented William John. Then he suddenly pulled off his mittens and held them out.

"Here – he can have mine. I'll get on without them well enough."

"Nonsense!" said Mrs. Ross, but less unkindly. "The fingers would freeze off you. Don't be a goose."

"It's all right," persisted Bertie. "I don't need them – much. And William John doesn't hardly ever get out."

He thrust them into her hand and ran quickly down the street, as though he feared that the keen air might make him change his mind in spite of himself. He had to stop a great many times that day to breathe on his purple hands. Still, he did not regret having lent his mittens to William John – poor, pale, sickly little William John, who had so few pleasures.

It was sunset when Bertie laid an armful of parcels down on the steps of Doctor Forbes's handsome house. His back was turned towards the big bay window at one side, and he was busy trying to warm his hands, so he did not see the two small faces looking at him through the frosty panes.

"Just look at that poor little boy, Amy," said the taller of the two. "He is almost frozen, I believe. Why doesn't Caroline hurry and open the door?"

"There she goes now," said Amy. "Edie, couldn't we coax her to let him come in and get warm? He looks so cold." And she drew her sister out into the hall, where the housekeeper was taking Bertie's parcels.

"Caroline," whispered Edith timidly, "please tell that poor little fellow to come in and get warm – he looks very cold."

"He's used to the cold, I warrant you," said the housekeeper rather impatiently. "It won't hurt him."

"But it is Christmas week," said Edith gravely, "and you know, Caroline, when Mamma was here she used to say that we ought to be particularly thoughtful of others who were not so happy or well-off as we were at this time."

Perhaps Edith's reference to her mother softened Caroline, for she turned to Bertie and said cordially enough, "Come in, and warm yourself before you go. It's a cold day."

Bertie shyly followed her to the kitchen.

"Sit up to the fire," said Caroline, placing a chair for him, while Edith and Amy came round to the other side of the stove and watched him with friendly interest.

"What's your name?" asked Caroline.

"Robert Ross, ma'am."

"Oh, you're Mrs. Ross's nephew then," said Caroline, breaking eggs into her cake-bowl, and whisking them deftly round. "And you're Sampson's errand boy just now? My goodness," as the boy spread his blue hands over the fire, "where are your mittens, child? You're never out without mittens a day like this!"

"I lent them to William John – he hadn't any," faltered Bertie. He did not know but that the lady might consider it a grave crime to be mittenless.

"No mittens!" exclaimed Amy in dismay. "Why, I have three pairs. And who is William John?"

"He is my cousin," said Bertie. "And he's awful sickly. He wanted to go out to play, and he hadn't any mittens, so I lent him mine. I didn't miss them – much."

"What kind of a Christmas did you have?"

"We didn't have any."

"No Christmas!" said Amy, quite overcome. "Oh, well, I suppose you are going to have a good time on New Year's instead."

Bertie shook his head.

"No'm, I guess not. We never have it different from other times."

Amy was silent from sheer amazement. Edith understood better, and she changed the subject.

"Have you any brothers or sisters, Bertie?"

"No'm," returned Bertie cheerfully. "I guess there's enough of us without that. I must be going now. I'm very much obliged to you."

Edith slipped from the room as he spoke, and met him again at the door. She held out a pair of warm-looking mittens.

"These are for William John," she said simply, "so that you can have your own. They are a pair of mine which are too big for me. I know Papa will say it is all right. Goodbye, Bertie."

"Goodbye – and thank you," stammered Bertie, as the door closed. Then he hastened home to William John.

That evening Doctor Forbes noticed a peculiarly thoughtful look on Edith's face as she sat gazing into the glowing coal fire after dinner. He laid his hand on her dark curls inquiringly.

"What are you musing over?"

"There was a little boy here today," began Edith.

"Oh, such a dear little boy," broke in Amy eagerly from the corner, where she was playing with her kitten. "His name was Bertie Ross. He brought up the parcels, and we asked him in to get warm. He had no mittens, and his hands were almost frozen. And, oh, Papa, just think! – he said he never had any Christmas or New Year at all."

"Poor little fellow!" said the doctor. "I've heard of him; a pretty hard time he has of it, I think."

"He was so pretty, Papa. And Edie gave him her blue mittens for William John."

"The plot deepens. Who is William John?"

"Oh, a cousin or something, didn't he say Edie? Anyway, he is sick, and he wanted to go coasting, and Bertie gave him his mittens. And I suppose he never had any Christmas either."

"There are plenty who haven't," said the doctor, taking up his paper with a sigh. "Well, girlies, you seem interested in this little fellow so, if you like, you may invite him and his cousin to take dinner with you on New Year's night."

"Oh, Papa!" said Edith, her eyes shining like stars.

The doctor laughed. "Write him a nice little note of invitation – you are the lady of the house, you know – and I'll see that he gets it tomorrow."

And this was how it came to pass that Bertie received the next day his first invitation to dine out.

He read the little note through three times in order fully to take in its contents, and then went around the rest of the day in deep abstraction as though he was trying to decide some very important question. It was with the same expression that he opened the door at home in the evening. His aunt was stirring some oatmeal mush on the stove.

"Is that you, Bert?" She spoke sharply. She always spoke sharply, even when not intending it; it had grown to be a habit.

"Yes'm," said Bertie meekly, as he hung up his cap.

"I s'pose you've only got one day more at the store," said Mrs. Ross. "Sampson didn't say anything about keeping you longer, did he?"

"No. He said he couldn't – I asked him."

"Well, I didn't expect he would. You'll have a holiday on New Year's anyhow; whether you'll have anything to eat or not is a different question."

"I've an invitation to dinner," said Bertie timidly, "me and William John. It's from Doctor Forbes's little girls – the ones that gave me the mittens."

He handed her the little note, and Mrs. Ross stooped down and read it by the fitful gleam of light which came from the cracked stove.

"Well, you can please yourself," she said as she handed it back, "but William John couldn't go if he had ten invitations. He caught cold coasting

yesterday. I told him he would, but he was bound
to go, and now he's laid up for a week. Listen to
him barking in the bedroom there."

"Well, then, I won't go either," said Bertie with
a sigh, it might be of relief, or it might be of disappointment. "I wouldn't go there all alone."

"You're a goose!" said his aunt. "They would-
n't eat you. But as I said, please yourself. Anyhow,
hold your tongue about it to William John, or you'll
have him crying and bawling to go too."

The caution came too late. William John had
already heard it, and when his mother went in to
rub his chest with liniment, she found him with the
ragged quilt over his head crying.

"Come, William John, I want to rub you."

"I don't want to be rubbed – g'way," sobbed
William John. "I heard you out there – you needn't
think I didn't. Bertie's going to Doctor Forbes's to
dinner and I can't go."

"Well, you've only yourself to thank for it,"
returned his mother. "If you hadn't persisted in
going out coasting yesterday when I wanted you
to stay in, you'd have been able to go to Doctor
Forbes's. Little boys who won't do as they're told
always get into trouble. Stop crying, now. I dare
say if Bertie goes they'll send you some candy, or
something."

But William John refused to be comforted. He cried himself to sleep that night, and when Bertie went in to see him next morning, he found him sitting up in bed with his eyes red and swollen and the faded quilt drawn up around his pinched face.

"Well, William John, how are you?"

"I ain't any better," replied William John mournfully. "I s'pose you'll have a great time tomorrow night, Bertie?"

"Oh, I'm not going since you can't," said Bertie cheerily. He thought this would comfort William John, but it had exactly the opposite effect. William John had cried until he could cry no more, but he turned around and sobbed.

"There now!" he said in tearless despair. "That's just what I expected. I did s'pose if I couldn't go you would, and tell me about it. You're mean as mean can be."

"Come now, William John, don't be so cross. I thought you'd rather have me home, but I'll go, if you want me to."

"Honest, now?"

"Yes, honest. I'll go anywhere to please you. I must be off to the store now. Goodbye."

Thus committed, Bertie took his courage in both hands and went. The next evening at dusk found him standing at Doctor Forbes's door with a very violently beating heart. He was carefully dressed in his well-worn best suit and a neat white collar. The frosty air had crimsoned his cheeks and his hair was curling round his face.

Caroline opened the door and showed him into the parlour, where Edith and Amy were eagerly awaiting him.

"Happy New Year, Bertie," cried Amy. "And – but, why, where is William John?"

"He couldn't come," answered Bertie anxiously – he was afraid he might not be welcome without William John. "He's real sick. He caught cold and has to stay in bed; but he wanted to come awful bad."

"Oh, dear me! Poor William John!" said Amy in a disappointed tone. But all further remarks were cut short by the entrance of Doctor Forbes.

"How do you do?" he said, giving Bertie's hand a hearty shake. "But where is the other little fellow my girls were expecting?"

Bertie patiently reaccounted for William John's non-appearance.

"It's a bad time for colds," said the doctor, sitting down and attacking the fire. "I dare say, though, you have to run so fast these days that a cold couldn't catch you. I suppose you'll soon be leaving Sampson's. He told me he didn't need you after the holiday season was over. What are you going at next? Have you anything in view?"

Bertie shook his head sorrowfully.

"No, sir; but," he added more cheerfully, "I guess I'll find something if I hunt around lively. I almost always do."

He forgot his shyness; his face flushed hopefully, and he looked straight at the doctor with his bright, earnest eyes. The doctor poked the fire energetically and looked very wise. But just then the girls came up and carried Bertie off to display their holiday gifts. And there was a fur cap and a pair of mittens for him! He wondered whether he was dreaming.

"And here's a picture-book for William John," said Amy, "and there is a sled out in the kitchen for him. Oh, there's the dinner-bell. I'm awfully hungry. Papa says that is my 'normal condition,' but I don't know what that means."

As for that dinner – Bertie might sometimes have seen such a repast in delightful dreams, but certainly never out of them. It was a feast to be dated from.

When the plum pudding came on, the doctor, who had been notably silent, leaned back in his chair, placed his finger-tips together, and looked critically at Bertie.

"So Mr. Sampson can't keep you?"

Bertie's face sobered at once. He had almost forgotten his responsibilities.

"No, sir. He says I'm too small for the heavy work."

"Well, you are rather small – but no doubt you will grow. Boys have a queer habit of doing that. I think you know how to make yourself useful. I need a boy here to run errands and look after my horse. If you like, I'll try you. You can live here, and go to school. I sometimes hear of places for boys in my rounds, and the first good one that will suit you, I'll bespeak for you. How will that do?"

"Oh, sir, you are too good," said Bertie with a choke in his voice.

"Well, that is settled," said the doctor genially. "Come on Monday then. And perhaps we can do something for that other little chap, William, or John, or whatever his name is. Will you have some more pudding, Bertie?"

"No, thank you," said Bertie. Pudding, indeed! He could not have eaten another mouthful after such wonderful and unexpected good fortune.

After dinner they played games, and cracked nuts, and roasted apples, until the clock struck nine; then Bertie got up to go.

"Off, are you?" said the doctor, looking up

from his paper. "Well, I'll expect you on Monday, remember."

"Yes, sir," said Bertie happily. He was not likely to forget.

As he went out Amy came through the hall with a red sled.

"Here is William John's present. I've tied all the other things on so that they can't fall off."

Edith was at the door with a parcel. "Here are some nuts and candies for William John," she said. "And tell him we all wish him a 'Happy New Year.'"

"Thank you," said Bertie. "I've had a splendid time. I'll tell William John. Goodnight."

He stepped out. It was frostier than ever. The snow crackled and snapped, the stars were keen and bright, but to Bertie, running down the street with William John's sled thumping merrily behind him, the world was aglow with rosy hope and promise. He was quite sure he could never forget this wonderful New Year.

Editorial Note

Except for the two Anne stories printed here, the other stories in this collection were originally published in the following magazines and newspapers, and are listed here in alphabetical order. Dates in square brackets are conjectural. Obvious typographical errors have been corrected, spelling and punctuation normalized.

Aunt Cyrilla's Christmas Basket, *Young People*, n.d. [1903?].

Bertie's New Year, *Pittsburgh Christian Advocate,* 28 December 1905, 10–12.

Christmas at Red Butte, *East and West*, 25 December 1909, 409–10.

A Christmas Inspiration, *Family Herald*, n.d. [1901?]; also in *Churchman*, 19 December 1909, 918-20.

A Christmas Mistake, *Family Herald*, 20 December 1899, 5. (This story was published within the last few years in a collection of Christmas tales by Canadian authors.)

The Christmas Surprise at Enderly Road, *King's Own*, 23 December 1905, 201–02.

Clorinda's Gifts, *Epworth Herald*, 15 December 1906, 731–32.

The End of the Young Family Feud, *Epworth Herald*, 14 December 1907, 743–45.

The Falsoms' Christmas Dinner, *East and West*, 22 December 1906, 401–02.

Ida's New Year Cake, *Days of Youth*, 31 December 1905, 2–3, 7.

The Josephs' Christmas, *Sunday School Visitor*, n.d. [1902].

Katherine Brooke Comes to Green Gables, *Anne of Windy Poplars* (1936), Second Year, sections 4–6, 162–87.

Matthew Insists on Puffed Sleeves, *Anne of Green Gables* (1908), ch. xxv, 271–85.

The Osbornes' Christmas, *Zion's Herald*, 16 December 1903, 1604–05.

Uncle Richard's New Year's Dinner, *Congregationalist*, 1 January 1910, 19–20. Also in *East and West*, 31 December 1910.

The Unforgotten One, *Zion's Herald*, 19 December 1906, 1619–20; also in *Canadian Courier*, 18 December 1909, 15, 23; and as She Was the Forgotten One, *Springfield Republican*, 22 December 1907, 24.

Other Books by L.M. Montgomery

The "Anne" Books (in order of Anne's life)

Anne of Green Gables, 1908
Anne of Avonlea, 1909
Anne of the Island, 1915
Anne of Windy Poplars, 1936
Anne's House of Dreams, 1917
Anne of Ingleside, 1939
Rainbow Valley, 1919
Rilla of Ingleside, 1920

The "Emily" Books

Emily of New Moon, 1923
Emily Climbs, 1925
Emily's Quest, 1927

Other Novels (in chronological order)

Kilmeny of the Orchard, 1910
The Story Girl, 1911
The Golden Road, 1913
The Blue Castle, 1926
Magic for Marigold, 1929
A Tangled Web, 1931
Pat of Silver Bush, 1933
Mistress Pat, 1935
Jane of Lantern Hill, 1937

Collections of Short Stories

Chronicles of Avonlea, 1912
Further Chronicles of Avonlea, 1920
The Road to Yesterday, 1974
The Doctor's Sweetheart, and Other Stories, 1979
Akin to Anne: Tales of Other Orphans, 1988
Along the Shore: Tales by the Sea, 1989
Among the Shadows: Tales from the Darker Side, 1990
After Many Days: Tales of Time Passed, 1991
Against the Odds: Tales of Achievement, 1993
At the Altar: Matrimonial Tales, 1994
Across the Miles: Tales of Correspondence, 1995

Poetry

The Watchman, and Other Poems, 1916
Poetry of Lucy Maud Montgomery, 1987